D0207022

REMEMBER
- TO -
REMEMBER

JIL PLUMMER

Andrew Benzie Books
Orinda, California

Published by Andrew Benzie Books
www.andrewbenziebooks.com

Printed in the United States of America

First Edition: January 2016

10 9 8 7 6 5 4 3 2 1

ISBN 978-1-941713-29-7

www.jilplummer.com

Cover and book design by Andrew Benzie

FOR MY FAMILY

Brenda (Chanbopha)

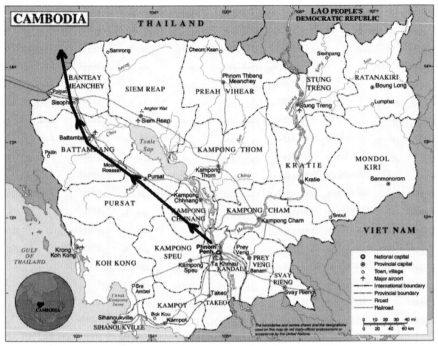

ROUTE TAKEN BY THE OUM FAMILY

POL POT

(from Wikipedia)

Pol Pot (19 May 1925–15 April 1998), born Saloth Sar, was a Cambodian revolutionary who led the Khmer Rouge from 1963 until 1997. From 1963 to 1981, he served as the General Secretary of the Communist Party of Kampuchea. As such, he became the leader of Cambodia on 17 April 1975, when his forces captured Phnom Penh. From 1976 to 1979, he also served as the prime minister of Democratic Kampuchea.

He presided over a totalitarian dictatorship, in which his government made urban dwellers move to the countryside to work in collective farms and on forced labour projects. The combined effects of executions, strenuous working conditions, malnutrition and poor medical care caused the deaths of approximately 25 percent of the Cambodian population. In all, an estimated 1 to 3 million people (out of a population of slightly over 8 million) died due to the policies of his four-year premiership.

In 1979, after the Cambodian–Vietnamese War, Pol Pot relocated to the jungles of southwest Cambodia, and the Khmer Rouge government collapsed. From 1979 to 1997, he and a remnant of the old Khmer Rouge operated near the border of Cambodia and Thailand, where they clung to power, with nominal United Nations recognition as the rightful government of Cambodia. Pol Pot died in 1998, while under house arrest by the Ta Mok faction of the Khmer Rouge. Since his death, rumours that he committed suicide or was poisoned have persisted.

PROLOGUE

During the course of each day we see strangers on the street, in shops and restaurants, on buses and trains. Some people we even meet often enough to say "hello" to, and subconsciously we evaluate them all. There's the pretty not very bright girl, wealthy gentleman, bimbo, conceited punk, emotionless janitor, uneducated gardener. How surprised we would often be to discover the truth behind those faces.

I am about to tell the story, as told to me by one whose inner strength and quick intelligence is hidden beneath the quiet exterior of the slight, smiling Cambodian woman who serves me my coffee each morning. Her name is Brenda. Once it was Chanbopha Oum.

CHAPTER ONE

Chanbopha was born in the bustling city of Phnom Penh, capital of Cambodia. At four years old she paid no attention to the distant gunfire which reminded adults of the civil war which had been raging across the country for the past five years. Instead she watched the street action from the window of her family's upper floor flat longing to be in the midst of all the laughter and chatter which floated up from what seemed a thrilling life of constant sunshine. There Tuk-Tuks, the bicycle taxis which towed passengers in their little carts, wove between the few private motor vehicles, buses, motorcycles, myriad bicycles and hand carts which flooded the road. Horns blared, bells rang while pedestrians rushed every which way in excitingly suicidal dashes. Sometimes there were accidents and people stood around waving their hands and arguing until traffic got moving again. Chan, as she was called by family, would laugh and shout unheard encouragement from her lofty perch.

The smells too were wonderful, especially of the fresh bread brought up each day to make a delicious breakfast dipped in a mix of warm water and evaporated milk. Chan may sometimes have longed for the time she was old enough to go outside alone but life was good in the apartment. She had siblings to play with; her three year old sister, Srey, her quiet seven year old brother, Sovirak, and Vuthy, an older boy Ma and Papa had adopted when his parents couldn't afford to feed him. His job was to look after Chan and she adored him almost as much as she did her soldier father who was also a professor of

1

Economics at Phnom Penh university. The four children would play hide and seek, skulking among the heavy antique furniture that had once belonged to their grandmother, and when they were allowed to polish the silver and brass ornaments it became a competition to see whose were the shiniest. Chan always won, same as she was first to learn the lessons taught by their strict tutor who came each afternoon. Eagerly she studied and could soon read almost anything she got her hands on, even if she didn't always understand the meaning.

That was how she first learned of the Khmer Rouge and a man called Pol Pot. She picked up the newspaper her parents had been frowning over the night before and spelled out those names. All she understood was that they had been fighting for years in the countryside outside Phnom Penh and a lot of people had been killed. When she went to Ma for information about which people and what "kill" meant, Ma avoided telling her and instead said not to worry because Pa and all his fellow soldiers were here to protect them. Now Chan really was worried and became more and more curious whenever her parents huddled over the radio and snapped it off when she entered the room.

Saturday was the best day of each week. It meant the park and freedom. She would cajole Vuthy into pushing her on the swing until she was dizzy, then she would run off to join games of tag with other children. They ran until they were puffed out and fell giggling to the grass.

On their way home Papa often stopped at a restaurant where she thrilled to see how people admired both him in his fine Captain's uniform and her beautiful mother. Chan enjoyed that almost as much as the curried chicken with noodles and luk lak. Life was a comfortable routine.

But that was before the one weekday when father came home early.

CHAPTER TWO

"Come, everyone. I have big, wonderful news!" Papa hadn't even removed the officer's cap which made him look so important and his brass buttons sparkled in a ray of sunshine that crept past the drapes. "I am honored to have been chosen by our king to attend Fort Eustis in the United States of America!" His uniformed chest puffed with pride.

What an honor, what joy! They all knew how Papa's marks had been top of everyone's in Military exams. Even the king had noticed! They clapped their hands and jumped around him, immensely proud and happy. Chan couldn't imagine why Mother didn't seem as thrilled as the rest of them nor why she stayed quiet for the rest of that day.

It seemed only a short time before Uncle was driving them to the airport in his grey town car, gliding like a ship through the chaos Chanbopha had so often watched from above. Now her nose smudged the glass as she reveled at being in the midst of it all. Then came the excitement of the airport: people rushing in every direction. Many foreigners, many uniforms. Chan's head spun as she tried to absorb it all. And only when she saw tickets being issued to Papa did she remember why they were there. He was really going to leave them. It wasn't just words and pride anymore. Chan clung to her father's sleeve and held on until the last moment when he was being told to go through a door away from them. Then he pried her fingers loose. She began to cry and he hoisted her up to face him. "It's only for six months. I trust you to look after your Ma especially well now; then later this year you'll have a new brother or sister to play with."

But I'm only five, she thought as he put her down and strode away. "Don't go! Don't go!" she called after him.

They were all crying now but he never looked back. Chan wondered if perhaps he was afraid that if he did he might cry too.

CHAPTER THREE

They were quiet on the way home. "When will Papa come back?" Chan ventured once only to be immediately hushed by Vuthy. Their city when they re-entered it seemed more filled with military than ever and Chan shuddered knowing that none of them was her father. Feeling naked and unprotected she buried her face in her Mother's sampot that January of 1975 and believed her soothing words that Papa would soon be home and there was nothing to worry about.

But Papa's return wasn't soon. It wasn't ever. Just three months after he'd left a cousin came to visit. She was a doctor and got to know things before anyone else.

This time she was bursting with news. "The French have gone. Helicopters in the night. You must telegraph your husband and tell him to stay in America. The Khmer Rouge will kill him if he comes here. Wire him immediately!" She paused for breath then Ma noticed Chan listening and bustled her out of the room.

Although she hadn't understood all the two women were talking about the name Khmer Rouge sent shivers running up and down Chan's spine and one thing that sent her heart plummeting was to know that Papa must not come back to Cambodia until something bad was over. She wanted to ask Ma what it was but knew she mustn't, so she just watched and listened.

She accompanied Vuthy to the wireless office later that day. There was a weirdness to the city. For one thing it was empty of the usual foreigners and local people moved quickly, only stopping to talk for short moments. There was no laughter. Soldiers were everywhere and military vehicles clogged the streets. Chanbopha found herself looking over her shoulder although she didn't know what for. She had to trot to keep up with her big brother who wouldn't slow down however she pleaded.

Ma waited by the door to let them in, her mouth pinched at the corners.

Yet indoors nothing seemed changed. The morning bread still arrived, their tutor still taught them and street sounds still rose to their window. Only the fact that she could no longer count the time till her father's return left a hollowness to Chan's days.

CHAPTER FOUR

Something was wrong. Chan sensed it from the way Ma spent hours listening to the radio. Neighbors and relatives arrived, talked in low voices, then rushed off. Chanbopha watched and worried, tried to eavesdrop but all she learned was that something terrible was about to happen although no one knew when. Ma didn't go shopping so their cupboards were becoming bare and meals boring. Chan woke up in the night to sounds of explosions and the hum of Ma's radio nearby. She developed tummy cramps from anxiety.

"Ma, it's Saturday. Can we go to the park?"

"No, we must stay inside today." Ma didn't usually snap like that. "You keep away from the windows too. Play with Srey."

Chan opened her mouth to argue that Srey was too young to be any fun, but something about the tightness of Ma's face made her go quiet and begin listening, picking out distant explosions and shouts; a hesitation in traffic sounds.

Chanbopha's heart seemed to miss a beat at the wail of sirens and the roar of low-flying aircraft. Perhaps all no different than on any other day-but then again…a shiver ran through her.

The streets of Phnom Penh were filled with joy. From her window Chanbopha looked down on the celebrating crowds. Laughing citizens danced around trucks and tanks loaded with grinning soldiers who wore pretty red scarves.

"Come away from there!" Ma roughly pulled Chan's arm.

"But it's a welcoming party. I heard them shout the war is over. A happy time, Ma, look!"

But Ma did not seem happy and the lines on her forehead were deep. Chan was confused. Her two brothers were probably out there and Ma had gone back to the radio. There was no one to ask, to explain. Papa could but he was in America. She remembered his parting words, "Now you look after your ma especially well." Chan had nodded acquiescence but now, two months later, she watched the happy crowds and felt only loneliness and confusion.

It was at four o'clock, on the morning of April seventeenth, 1975, when the building shuddered and the repetitive crack of machine guns shocked Chanbopha awake. Bolting upright, she stared into darkness. Noise beat at her; screams, shouts for help, running feet, pounding boots, gun shots, the deep throated rumble of an explosion close by. A baby wailed and went too suddenly silent. Chan couldn't breathe. What was happening? She didn't understand. Men's voices shouted orders. Strange thuds followed. Children wailed and called for parents. Parents called for children. I must wake up. I must, she thought. Then Ma was beside her with Srey, her little sister, and Sovirak, her brother. "Shhh! Be quiet," Ma hissed. "We must hide 'til it's over."

"Where's Vuthy?" asked Chan.

"Shhh!" said Ma and the four of them huddled on Chan's bed.

Hammering on the street door far below startled them. It reverberated through the house. Men's voices commanded, "Out! Now! Everyone! You disobey, we kill."

They huddled closer. Srey whimpered and Ma put her hand over the child's mouth. "It's the Khmer Rouge," she whispered. "Pol Pot's soldiers."

"But all that rejoicing... they said the war was over!" Chanbopha had her lips close to Ma's ear.

"But sometimes the wrong side wins," said Ma. "Now hush."

"All out!" The voice was closer. Maybe on the second floor. A burst of gunfire. A scream abruptly cut off.

"Ma, Ma, we must go!" Chanbopha's whisper was hoarse with terror.

A figure burst through the bedroom door. It was Vuthy, the eldest boy "What are you doing here?" He grasped the sleeve of Ma's night gown. "Quick! We must leave. Now!"

"No. I will not abandon my home; the antiques left by my grandmother!" Ma tore her wrist away from Vuthy's grip. "I'll not go. Nobody can make me leave what is mine!"

"If you stay you will painfully be sent to join your dead grandmother. You and your children. Do you want that? Come! Now! Take nothing of value. We must look poor. Not even reading glasses. You've heard what they do. Come on!"

Chan felt her big "brother's" urgency and saw through darkness terror on Ma's face and indecision in her eyes.

Chan trusted Vuthy most next to Papa. He was right. "Go!" she screamed and began beating on Ma's leg with her small fists. "Go! Go! Go!"

Immediately everyone was running to get dressed and in moments they gathered by the stairs. Ma had on a long yellow skirt and white blouse. Chan had climbed into the yellow shorts and tank top she had worn earlier, and struggled to put on the American wristwatch Papa had sent her.

Vuthy grabbed it out of her hand. "If they see this they will think you a rich child. They'll kill you-us too!"

Tears filled Chan's eyes. "But Papa..."

Vuthy smiled at her and gently took the watch. "I will hide this where no Pol Pot will find it. It will be safe and so will you. Okay?"

Chanbopha nodded slowly. She trusted Vuthy. "Hold hands," he ordered. "Now! We must go!"

And they did, Sovirak with Ma at one end of their little chain and Chan between Ma and Vuthy who carried Srey on his back.

It was like being devoured by a gigantic serpent when they entered the street and were sucked into the belly of churning, overwhelming terror.

CHAPTER FIVE

Chan ran trapped in a jungle of legs and submerged in a roar of movement, wails and cries. She stumbled and jumped over fallen bodies being dragged by relatives Dogs dashed, lost and panic-eyed. One man carried a turtle. People pushed barrows filled with belongings, rode bicycles loaded with bags and pushed motor cycles and cars which could not be driven through the crush. Many clutched bundles, balanced more on their heads and hugged bawling babies under an arm. Young soldiers drove army vehicles alongside; boys or girls, Chan couldn't tell which for with their short hair, Mao caps, identical black uniforms and red checkered scarves they all looked male. One perched on an elephant, rifle across his knees. In horror Chan watched a tank run over a child who had strayed from his parents. It might have been the same one who had danced a joyous welcome when the Khmer Rouge drove into the city just the day before. Chan had seen all that celebrating. What had happened? How could a wrong side win like ma said.

Some soldiers laughed as one leaned to slash the neck of an old woman who had collapsed, her toothless mouth open as she gasped for breath. Now her head rolled among the running feet. Any bicycle spotted and easily grabbed was snatched from its owner and flung against a wall to lie a crumpled skeleton amongst others. Explosions and the smells of gunpowder, sweat and urine. Screams and shouts, death and blood. There was no time to think as Chanbopha gripped the hands of her Ma and Vuthy terrified of losing them. They just ran and ran-forever.

At one time, when her short legs were so tired they barely held her up, a stranger sat Chan on some bulging sacks balanced on the bicycle he had managed so far to keep. Although for a while it was a great relief she was glad when he put her back on the ground and she again held the hands of her family.

A loud explosion shook the ground as they left the city and rumor spread that the Pol Pot had blown up the central bank.

Paved road turned to dirt and gravel and the pace slowed. Chan had lost one sandal but didn't notice the soreness of her foot until they stopped and sat on a patch of grass. By the height of the sun it must have been noon and she watched as people took out food they had brought. Why, with all the radio listening and whispering in past weeks, hadn't Ma prepared something too? Had she just been too stubbornly intent on staying in her home to have considered another outcome? "You are hungry, little one?" The man next to them smiled and pulled a live chicken from under his jacket. Chan watched while he snapped its neck and plucked its feathers; others made a fire over which the bird soon cooked. Now the air, which had recently reeked of unbreathable stenches, filled with the aroma of cooked meat. Gratefully the family and a few hapless others shared their new friend's generosity.

"Ma, why are the soldiers so mean?" asked Chan as she watched one swagger past, chewing on a rice cake he had just snatched from the hand of a small boy.

"They are uneducated country people who have never known kindness; not even from their parents. You see their dark skin from working in the sun? Pol Pot took their empty minds and hearts and filled them with poison." Ma wiped her hands on some feathers then told Chan to do the same. "Be careful. They must never know about Papa being an officer in the Cambodian army. Or that any of us are educated or can even read. They must believe we lived in a poor place not our fine apartment. Listen carefully, Child. Do you understand?" Ma stared into Chanbopha's eyes, willing her to be silent about all the things she was proud of. "They are very dangerous, little

Chan. Pol Pot puffed up their pride until their conscience died. That is the most frightening thing about these soldiers. They have no conscience." They sat in silence while a young mother suckled her baby nearby. "Now, go to the river and fill these bottles," Ma, waved toward willows from which people appeared with flasks and sloshing containers.

"Yes, Ma." Chan felt better now her tummy was full and she refused to show the pain from her blistered foot as she passed clusters of people who rested in disheveled heaps as far as she could see.

CHAPTER SIX

The water when she reached it was an inlet off the Mekong river which they had been following all morning and it rippled, cool and inviting, blocking out the chaos of the outside world. As if to wash away the least vestige of the last twenty four hours, Chan put down her bottles and jumped in. It didn't matter that she had never been allowed to swim or play in a pool for as she dove beneath the surface she became a mermaid from one of Ma's folk tales, and all the dust, sweat and confusion fell away. Then she drank until the thirst she hadn't known she had was quenched. The water felt natural to her and she loved how her hair floated behind her, released from the ribbons which usually held it in two bunches. She blew bubbles and laughed, and splashed.

The lagoon was not deep and after a time she stood up smiling and listening to a bird, the only sound to break the silence. So quiet.

Too quiet!

Chan scrambled up the bank, forgetting her one sandal, and looked out between the willows toward the road. Empty. Nobody. They'd left her! Away in the distance she saw what seemed like a black cloud, slowly receding. "Ma!" The humid heat of mid-day muffled Chanbopha's cries. "Ma! Ma! Wait for me! Wait!" She began to run as fast as she could but that soon dropped to a walk, then a shuffle. Her clothes were already dry and dirtier than before her swim, dust having formed into muddy streaks. Head down, hair straggling into her eyes, she saw only well-trodden dirt swirling around her bare feet and was careful not to look at dark shapes at the side of the road lest she recognize them for the dead she suspected they were. On and on. Ma, Ma why don't you wait? She wanted to sit down, right where she was, and sob her despair and panic but instead she kept moving. Papa will be proud some day, she told herself over and over.

Chan sneezed as familiar rank smells clogged her nose. She stumbled and almost fell onto something soft. It was a bundle being dragged behind an old man or woman, impossible to tell which. Chan had reached the tail of the fleeing mass of people. With renewed energy she fought her way through all the wheels, knees, legs and bleeding feet. Few paid any heed as, sounding like an orphaned lamb, she bleated, "Ma! Vuthy! Wait for me!"

Her voice joined all the others, wailing, sobbing, weakly now for everyone was hot and tired, barely able to move but knowing if they stopped it would be the end for them. The harsh barking Khmer Rouge who drove alongside killed more often as the day wore on, sometimes crushing people under rubber tires, leaving them to writhe in agony until death rescued them. Chan barely noticed the dead faces and contorted bodies she passed. So many. Too many to care. All that mattered was finding Ma.

The road split and, unbeknownst to her, her family had taken the top fork while she blindly followed those on the bottom. She trotted zigzagging through the endless parade of misery. Despair and hopelessness were so overwhelming she was no longer aware of her own whimpers. Several people wanted to help and asked her to walk with them but she barely noticed and they, watching her stumble past, pulled their own children closer.

"Chanbopha!" A hand fell on her shoulder and swung her around.

"Oh, Vuthy." It came out as a whisper but in Chan's heart it was a shout as she flung her arms around the waist of her dear adopted brother. They faced back into the crowd, fighting the current but staying in the middle so the Khmer Rouge wouldn't notice them. Vuthy almost carried his little charge back to where the road divided, then up onto the top fork where not far along Ma, Srey and Sovirak waited. "Chan!" Ma's voice stopped her from blindly passing.

With her face pressed against her mother's knees Chanbopha choked on dry sobs. "I forgot the water!" she whimpered.

"No worry!" Ma grasped her daughter's hand as they were once again swept along in the tide of refugees.

CHAPTER SEVEN

The pain of Ma's grip crushing her fingers was the best feeling in the world to little Chan and now her bare feet no longer hurt although they still left specks of blood on the road behind her.

They walked for four days and at first kind people shared supplies and water with those who had none, but by the end of the second day there was little to spare and people guarded what they had for their own families. The Oums picked fruit off trees they passed and bought rice and other foods from villagers eager to take advantage of the "new people" as evicted city dwellers were now called.

The sides of the road were strewn with belongings owners could no longer carry. Among them, more and more often, were the elderly or ill unable to continue and so left behind to die.

At night, exhausted, the Oums curled together on whatever empty piece of grass they could find and although Chan ached all over she immediately tumbled into the black mercy of sleep.

Late afternoon on the fourth day this huge human migration left the road for a lane that ended in front of a high barbed wire gate. They had been travelling since before dawn. Most were exhausted, many were no longer present, either having been slaughtered for displaying some sign of bourgeoisie wealth or education, or been overtaken by weakness. In any case, they would never be seen again.

As Chan waited, events of the past days replayed in her mind, stirring up a great loathing for the soldiers in their red scarves. She had never felt this emotion before and she didn't know what to do with it but she swore to herself that somehow she would get her family through this and back to Papa. He would show these Khmer Rouge what a real army officer was!

For now she concentrated on helping Ma find water for little sister Srey, then a patch of ground for them to rest on. The heat was damp and oppressive. Srey and Ma, who worried about the child in her belly, went quickly to sleep. At each of their previous stops Chan had sought food and drink but this time she sat with Vuthy and Sovirak fighting to stay awake in order to catch the words of the Pol Pot officer who was screaming instructions. She wondered if these strange soldiers even knew how to talk like ordinary people. Maybe they really were the storybook monsters she had imagined when she first heard Ma mention them. And their cruel king, Pol Pot, where was he? Chan shivered and shook the thoughts from her head as she struggled to understand what the officer was saying. "All hair must be cut same short length. All equal in good communist way." Surely she had misunderstood!

They were divided into groups, each of which was placed under the command of a soldier guard. Chan saw that the one assigned to them looked very young, not much older than Vuthy, but his expression was mean and his eyes hard as marbles. Her back stiffened and she knew she would hate everything he said.

He roughly herded them through the gates into what seemed a village of A-shaped roofs. Chan's family was shoved toward one of these wall-less huts and as they clustered in the doorway looking at the dirt floor Chan's heart sank. There was nothing— not even a bed or a table. Were the five of them really to live in this small miserable space? Srey began to wail. "This dirty, nasty place. I not stay here." Her howls grew louder.

"Hush, the guards will come!" Just that day Chanbopha had seen terrible punishments done in retaliation for quieter complaints than this-people's heads cracked open with the butt of a rifle; beatings that soaked clothing red. "Ma! Ma!" She tugged at her mother's arm. Frantic. Pleading. "Ma. Ma. Make her quiet. Please." Then, understanding that her mother was too weary to do anything, Chan knelt in front of her little sister and took hold of her small hands. "Srey baby. We will make nice beds. We will make a game and see who can gather the most ferns, branches or grass and they will be soft and sweet to sleep on. Come everyone."

"Chan is right." said Vuthy. "Come, the edge of the jungle is close. Let's get there before others have the same idea."

Because Srey adamantly refused to come with them, repeating over and over that the ground was dirty, they laid her on a sack someone had dropped and covered her with any clothing they could spare to keep her safe from mosquitos. Immediately, thumb in mouth, she slept.

How Chan wished they had machetes as the tall grass sliced her fingers. She could hear the two boys ripping branches and matting off palms while she and her mother piled their own collection of anything that grew even remotely soft. At last there was enough and they were exhausted.

It was getting dark as they dragged it all back and into their hut. People had looked out to see what was happening and Chanbopha heard muttering and soon the padding of feet as neighbors headed for the jungle, following the Oum family's example. After only a few moments the voice of a guard bellowed, commanding prisoners back to their huts. A rifle cracked. "Animals sleep on ground. You no better. You lucky to have roof!"

Sounds of running. Then quiet.

Chanbopha, Ma, Vuthy and Sovirak very quietly trampled and bunched their own piles into two thick beds. Chan imagined how, after Papa rescued them, someone would tell him this had been her idea. He would smile and be proud of his daughter.

"Before we sleep you must cut our hair," said Sovirak, handing Ma the sharp knife he always carried. "We must allow no excuses for these Pol Pot to give us what they call punishment."

And Ma got to work, hacking as best she could so everyone's hair stopped short at the nape of their neck. Even Srey's, although she was too sleepy to notice. Chan felt tears stinging inside her nose as the black strands she had brushed so diligently each night in Phnom Penh dropped onto the ground around her; but when Ma handed the knife to Sovirak to cut her own hair, styled each month until now in the most expensive hair salon in the city, Chan had to turn away.

She felt Ma's hand on hers. "It will grow again," Ma said in that soft voice she used to soothe a hurt child.

"Yes, Ma, I know we must play the game to get back to Pa." Chanbopha bent to collect the soft black pile from the ground. "I will make it into a pillow for Srey,"

Vuthy handed her a large handkerchief. "And here is the pillow case." he said.

After Chan wrapped all the hair in the material, the four of them slipped it under the sleeping child's head.

Family is all that matters, thought Chan, and what's a little hair anyway?

Too tired to even feel hungry, she lay down next to Ma who already slept beside Srey. The breathing of the boys in the other bed became deep and regular and the camp lay silent.

CHAPTER EIGHT

Chanbopha awoke as dawn slivered through the gap between roof and floor. Quickly she closed her eyes lest her nightmare about the previous day proved to be real. But pictures insisted on scrolling through her mind—the tumult, the panicked crowds, the beatings and beheadings, the heat. Soldiers laughing as one of them with a sharpened bamboo sword pierced a baby in its mother's arms. Chan whimpered, her eyes shot open and her body was so tense she ached. "Oh, Papa," she whispered.

A loudspeaker bellowed for them to get up, saying it was four thirty and calling them lazy scum. Anyone late would be beaten.

Srey refused to get off the bed to walk to the nearby trees to relieve herself so Chan carried her piggyback. Returned to their hut, the small child dug deep back into the bed and refused to budge further.

"Here, we must wear these. A soldier brought them." Ma handed Chan a pair of shorts and a t-shirt. It was all black, rough cotton. Ma already wore the long pants and top given to her. Then Vuthy and Sovirak appeared and Chan flinched for they wore the same uniform of black pants and t-shirt as the Pol Pot and for a moment that's who she thought they were.

She turned back to her mother who was desperately trying to coax Srey off the bed. "Leave her." Chan was surprised to hear her voice ordering Ma so sharply but she knew it was necessary. Her recent nightmare had reinforced her understanding of the horrors these Khmer Rouge were only too willing to perform.

"She's too young to work and if she fusses they'll beat her. We must leave her here."

Ma looked ready to argue, then shrugged, and the four of them joined the other prisoners in the compound outside.

Everyone wore the same kind of black outfit, the only difference being that children wore shorts, everyone else had long pants. Chan did wish they had at least been given the red scarves the soldiers had. Most prisoners had cut their hair and those who hadn't were called out and subjected to a barbarous hacking which left their scalps with no more covering than that of a mangy street dog.

First women were put into one group; men, which included Sovirak and Vuthy, in another, and children in the third.

Chanbopha turned to the plump girl next to her. "Where are we..." but before she could finish a bamboo pole crashed against her left ear and the guard screamed into her face. She watched his spittle fly and felt it on her cheek.

"You do not speak. You do not look at each other. Never!" The pole slashed again, across Chan's shoulder this time so she almost fell. "Never. You hear?"

The other children cowered.

"Follow!" The guard led them along a path through jungle which snuffed what there was of morning light until they came to the edge of rough fields.

Water buffalo grazed as early mist rose around them.

"You pick up dung. Pile on cart there in corner. Later you return to camp to eat. After that, you come back to this field and collect more dung or go to the rice paddy and pick weeds or rice thinnings."

Chanbopha could feel the child next to her shivering and out of the corners of her eyes saw that most of the girls and boys were older, maybe nine or ten. They would expect her to be weaker and bear the brunt of sadistic soldiers' actions. Well, she might be small but she was the proud daughter of an officer who had received honor from the king. Chan pulled her shoulders back and ran off into the field to prove she could fill her arms with more of the smelly stuff, more often, than anyone else. The big animals paid no attention to the children and went on with their grazing however close the humans got. As the temperature rose the herd moved to a boggy pond in a far corner and Chan, hearing them snort and splash, envied them.

Heat suffocated like being inside a furnace. As morning progressed Chan's back ached and her eyes stung with sweat. She could barely see and she struggled to stay upright while others collapsed. The thunk of the guard's bamboo as he tried to get them back on their feet made her even more adamant not to provide any excuse for him to notice her. He struck many and often but never her.

The sun was almost straight above when they filed in for their first meal. The line at the kitchen doorway was long and when her turn came Chanbopha grasped the tin bowl handed her, desperate to quell the hunger cramps in her stomach. She hurried to a corner of the compound and sat on bare ground with her back against a wall before taking a sip of the hot soup.

She spluttered and almost spat it out. Hot, nasty water with eight (she counted them) grains of rice floating disconsolately near the bottom. She almost threw it on the ground. Was this all they were supposed to live on? How could Ma and little Srey survive on this? She knew she couldn't.

At that moment Chan recognized her mother entering the compound. Was that bent, black clad creature shuffling past with a tin bowl in one hand, really the smartly dressed, and proud, officer's wife of only five days earlier? "Ma?"

The relief in those tired eyes as she turned made Chan leap to her feet and run to the woman she had so seldom hugged but now they clung to each other as though they had never expected to meet again.

Amazingly Ma spilled none of her soup.

"Where are you going with that ?" asked Chan.

"Little Srey must eat. She refuses to step on the ground. Says it's dirty. I don't know why she behaves this way. I've tried everything but she refuses and they only give food to those who come here and get their own ration."

"But you must eat too."

"My child is most important." She shrugged. "What am I to do?"

Chan glanced at the shuffling line of weary people. "You take that to Srey and then come back. I will get soup for you. They'll not recognize a same small girl going through more than once."

And they didn't. In fact from then on Chanbopha would make many return trips for extra soup for her family, sometimes wondering why none of them would help her by trying the same trick.

On this first day, however, Chan felt elated to have found one way to help them survive in this camp and she, then and there, made it her goal to find others.

Break time over, after too short a rest, the children were sent to the rice fields where they must pull weeds and the weaker rice seedlings from rows of those growing into stronger plants. At first the mud around Chan's feet felt good but soon, as the sun continued to beat down, it just felt slippery and difficult. At the other end of the paddy adults were only bent-over shapes and she wondered if Ma was one them. The boys and men worked at cutting back jungle to make the farm bigger. Ma had found that out during the break.

CHAPTER NINE

Chan's hands blistered and she moved like an automaton, wondering if this day would ever end. A girl near her fainted and lay in the mud. Immediately a guard ran over shouting. He began to beat her savagely. The girl screamed once then was quiet. She was still lying there, face down when they were ordered back to camp and the soup they were almost too tired to drink. In their hut Chanbopha, ignoring Srey's complaints, pushed her aside and curled into a tight ball. Ma and the boys returned later when it was almost dark and all fell into bed without speaking. Everyone suffered from insect bites, cuts and scratches. Vuthy had a slash across one cheek and no one asked how he got it.

Day followed day. Week followed week. Body followed body to the graveyard in the newly cleared patch of jungle. Often one would lie putrefying in the hot sun until soldiers ordered a group of prisoners to move it. Chan barely noticed them anymore. One morning the loud speaker announced that Cambodia was no more. Now the country's name was Kampuchea and, as was befitting the start of Communist rule, the calendar would begin with year one. Chan remembered the bustling streets she used to look down on from their apartment window. Remembered the voices and laughter she had delighted to hear. Remembered the smell of new bread. Where had it all gone? What had happened!

That night, for the first time Chan heard her mother sob.

Old, weak and very young died from malnutrition and dysentery. Ma said each died of a broken heart. Feet rotted from the constant mud of the rice paddy. Chanbopha's arms and legs were covered in open sores. She had been given a pair of the tire tread sandals worn by the Pol Pot but they were painful so she was better off barefoot. A wound opened on her right instep, so walking changed to a hobble, and mud caused deep cracks between her toes.

There was nowhere to bathe except in the nearby pond caused by overflow from the passing river, but it was filthy from so many people using it and Chan often felt dirtier when she got out than when she went in. Then arrived the first downpour of the monsoon season. Everyone ran outside, letting the warm deluge scour their bodies and bug infested hair. They even spread their clothes out to be washed by nature and for a few moments the prisoners forgot their misery and some even smiled.

If Chan had one wish it would be to jump out of her itching, throbbing skin.

Ma pleaded for some ointment from the camp's doctor but he sent her away saying there was only enough for the soldiers. That night Ma disappeared into the jungle and returned with some Tamarind leaves which she boiled and used to bathe Chan's foot. Then she made a paste from crushed herbs and spread it over all the other sores and irritations on herself and her children. "My grandmother told me about this," she said. "I hope I remember right."

Oh, what relief Chan felt with that unguent soothing her arms and legs and back. Then in the wound of her foot. The sores didn't go away and the mosquitoes kept biting but the fevered agony dissipated and the whole family escaped the continuing misery which drove many in the camp close to madness.

To stop from thinking of the horrors rampant around her, Chanbopha crammed her mind with ways to help her family survive. That meant food. And food was anything that moved; the rats that squealed in the thatch at night were caught and pulled down by their tails, then killed by the boys. Snails and frogs from the pond were smuggled in to be added to soup heated over the small fire made in the tin can Chan stole from the kitchen trash pile. Chan also stole matches from their chain smoking guard while he was smacking the face of a boy he had caught stealing a green banana as they passed on their way to the field. She felt good later when she saw the brutal soldier cursing and fruitlessly searching with an unlit cigarette dangling from his lip. Bugs and juicy caterpillars were added to the stew. But it was never enough and they were always hungry. When Ma's secretly planted bananas were almost ripe, she returned one day to find them all ripped and gone from their stem.

Everyone tried to sneak fruit in from the jungle and even stole from each other. One day when Ma arrived home with her back covered in mud she told how she had hidden a beautiful ripe mango under her shirt. "I thought no one would notice," she told Chan. "You know—with the baby showing."

Chan had noticed the baby was making it difficult for Ma to fasten her trousers.

"One of the other workers saw the mango. He was envious and told the guard who shouted and roughly grabbed me. Then he pushed me so hard I fell into a ditch and the mango disappeared." Ma's eyes glistened. "People are getting mean, Chan. Trust no one."

Because they had to be more careful after that, they were all losing weight—especially Vuthy and Sovirak who did hard manual labor from dawn to dark.

There were no more rats left in the thatch and insects took too much energy to catch for the miniscule nutrition they provided. Chanbopha still caught small creatures among the rice stalks but the ache in her belly never let her forget her fight against hunger.

CHAPTER TEN

Chan learned to tune out many things and one was the sound of screams that often came from the building at the end of the compound next to the bamboo house where the soldiers lived. Once she saw a palm frond on the porch, its serrated edge covered in blood, and she ran home, her teeth chattering from ghastly imaginings.

Srey escaped the mosquito and bug bites by staying in bed, lightly covered but still she complained continuously: about the heat, her empty stomach, although she barely ate what was given her, and the dirt. Chanbopha tried to explain how they couldn't change things, mustn't upset Ma, but little Srey wouldn't or couldn't, understand. She just seemed to get more and more stubborn, even refusing the soup Ma coaxed her to drink. Sometimes Chan wanted to shake some sense into her. Even slap her, but she never did. Ma never sang now. No one did.

Ma and Chan took to sneaking into the jungle early, before anyone was up, to find herbs and mushrooms to add to whatever else they got that day. At one time thought of entering such an alien world of tangled vines, trees and unknown creatures would have terrified city bred Chanbopha but now the land of the Khmer Rouge was far more frightening.

When they got home after a successful hunt they didn't mention that the bits of meat in that night's soup were a nest of baby mice they'd found, or even adult mice when they were lucky; or when the plump mouthfuls were fat grubs from a rotten tree trunk.

Every day when Chanbopha passed the kitchens on her way to and from the rice paddies she paused to breathe in the sweet smell of real food. Often the cooks would be sitting on the steps smoking, ignoring passersby, and Chan wondered if they were ordered not to speak to the prisoners or just didn't like them. But this evening was different.

"Smell good, little one?" said a woman she'd never seen before.

"Very good," said Chan. "You must be fine cooks!"

"Come, the floor needs sweeping," A voice shrilled from the open doorway.

"Ohh," moaned the woman on the step. "Just a little longer."

"Let me! I like to sweep," said Chan, trying to look eager and not at all tired after her long day in the fields.

The woman took a drag on her cigarette, looked Chan up and down, shrugged, then nodded in the direction of the kitchen.

Chan ran inside where a replica of the first woman, who like everyone else wore the uniform black pants and black top, stood with a broom. "What's your name, Child?"

"Chan."

"Okay, little Chan. One worker got sick last week and sent away. You small but any help good."

Chanbopha knew the guards ate well. She had smelled their meals being prepared apart from the pots of rice soup simmering for the prisoners. She remembered that once grown-ups had considered her small and cute and now she hoped she could still use that to sneak into the affections of the harried kitchen staff. She emptied garbage without being asked and was there to mop when something was spilled. She ran to wipe up spattered grease.

"Good girl!" a skinny older woman patted her on the head and, perhaps remembering grandchildren not seen for a long time, paused and gave a toothless smile. "You hungry?"

Chan looked up filling her face with as much longing as possible and opening brown eyes their biggest as she nodded vehemently.

"Well child, you help me and you will have food. I have vegetables to prepare and these old hands just won't do it more. Come."

In another part of the kitchen the smells of real food made Chanbopha's stomach clench and her head go faint so she was relieved when the old woman sat her down on a bench with a pile of vegetables which she must scrub in the nearby bucket of water then slice for cooking. For a while Chan worked diligently all the time fighting temptation to stuff her mouth and pockets full. At last the huge pile was gone leaving Chan's fingers covered with nicks for she had never been allowed to do such work at home. In a way she was proud not to have cut off any fingers such as Ma had warned happened to small children who played with knives. The old woman was pleased and asked Chan to stir rice cooking in a huge pot. "Don't let it stick," she warned before going outside to smoke a foul smelling cigarette. After a while the woman came in and sat on the bench watching her.

"Do you have children?" Chanbopha ventured.

"Ah, yes. Many beautiful babies. All grown and gone."

"Tell me about them."

And the old woman did, remembering each one as he, for they all seemed to be boys, worked on that small farm on the edge of a far off jungle. "Now the food is ready and the soldiers will soon be here to eat." She stood up and found a pot which she filled with chicken, vegetables, rice and noodles. She draped a cloth over it. "Thank you, Chan, child. Come back tomorrow if you can. And don't get caught or I…" she ran a kitchen knife across her throat.

Chanbopha carried her treasure back to the hut. Vuthy and Sovorik had just arrived tired and dirty. Ma had come in a little earlier and was becoming concerned about Chan's absence.

"Where have you been?" She demanded as soon as she saw her daughter. "Bad girl to make me worry so!"

The boys had followed their noses to the good smell and whisked the cover off the pot Chan hugged to her chest.

"Food—real food!" whispered Sovirak.

They all stood looking as though it were a mirage they expected might vanish at their least twitch.

"Get your bowls. We must eat before someone finds out," said Ma.

And they did, not pausing until each last morsel was swallowed. Ma had taken some to Srey but she wrinkled her nose and nibbled one tiny strip of chicken before turning her head away.

"I think she's forgotten how to eat, only drinks now," said Ma sadly.

In this way Chan's family stayed stronger than most of those around them. Except for Srey who became weaker, only staying alive due to Ma forcing mostly soup into her mouth.

CHAPTER ELEVEN

The Pol Pot had slacked off on their night patrols which allowed Ma to secretly connect with other family members in the camp including her own mother who, too old to work, helped look after Srey during the day. Several aunties[1] also visited after work, flitting silently through the dark like moths to talk and wonder what had happened to their husbands.

Chanbopha was bored. Same routine, everyone like a skeleton, wearing black and looking miserable. Children never played or laughed, just skinny and crying. Each morning the same loud speaker at dawn. Same ugly, ragged, smelly clothes, never clean however often they were scrubbed in the river which she suspected only made them smellier. She did now have some dead child's sandals she tied to her feet with vines because the straps were broken. First came a dash to the jungle, luckily washed clean each night by heavy rains, holding Srey who adamantly refused to touch the ground while she relieved herself of very little. Then off to collect dung in the fields. Chan sometimes tried to talk to other girls but they ducked their heads and stayed silent, too many beatings and hunger having broken any spirit they once may have had. It frustrated Chan that they were so cowed. She relished even the smallest of her victories over their mean soldier guards and she still heard Pa's last words to her. "Look after your Ma."

---

[1] *In Cambodia the term "Auntie" is used by children for any female adult regardless of blood-tie*

Every evening, on her way home from the rice paddy, Chan slipped unnoticed from the group of tired children, and worked in the kitchen. The staff depended on her to do many of their chores for them, often saving their heaviest for her arrival. Did they treat their own children like this, she often wondered as she scrubbed pans or struggled out with garbage. But she was thankful for the food she got in return, some they gave and some she stole, although however much she got to take back to her family it was never enough.

That walk home was something she dreaded: first was fear of being seen by a guard but even worse was having to pass that terrible hut from which screams often made shivers run through her, from her tail bone to the top of her head, and sometimes she had to stop herself from screaming too.

One night she overheard her brothers whispering about that place. Words like torture, beatings and fingernails being pulled out. "Today, Just because the man took for himself his dead wife's soup." Chanbopha knew it must be true, after seeing children beaten and killed in the fields for the slightest offense.

Pol Pot soldiers always watched, eager to inflict pain or worse. She wondered why. Was it sport to them as tricking them had become a game for her? Did they compare numbers of prisoners they had brutalized during the day? Perhaps for getting food in secret such as she was doing while unseen in the kitchen between dishing out their noodles?

Chan became ever more cunning; each day's reward being to reach her bed at night still safe, and her whole family, except for Srey, sleeping with something in their bellies.

Ma had gotten too big with the baby to help much so Chanbopha went alone into the early dawn looking for anything edible to add to what she brought from the kitchen. She had grown to like being in the jungle. It seemed a parallel world where she could pause to admire shimmering cobwebs strung across her path proving that no one else had lately come this way. Here it was safe to hum a tune her mother used to sing in the "before" time and she would talk to the red and yellow parrot who cocked a beady eye at her as he preened his feathers. Monkeys with round eyed babies clinging to their backs ran along branches looking down at her and Chan became lost in their carefree, joyous overhead existence.

She had to force herself to go back to the hut where Srey whined constantly. Chan could only think that the rout from Phnom Penh had traumatized her little sister and damaged her brain. Why would she not set a foot on the ground which was clean inside their one room? Ma had even made a broom out of coconut fronds. Srey weighed almost nothing and was hollow eyed and strange looking. Sometimes Chan was afraid to look at her. She tried to remember what the little one had been like before, but couldn't. What if she completely forgot everything about before!

The kitchen women sat outside smoking and gossiping much of the time while Chan did their work for them. She couldn't ignore that her efforts seemed unappreciated and that her brothers did little to help, that Srey was so difficult, occupying all Ma's attention and that the baby's time was coming close. She didn't know if she could manage another mouth to feed. But she must keep everyone safe for Papa. Only then could she rest.

She stopped her secret trips into the jungle.

No one seemed kind anymore. People who had helped during their exodus from the city, even relatives, were too tired and afraid; too hungry and sick to care about anyone but themselves. In the soup line Chan had seen a woman steal an old man's just filled bowl and gulp the liquid down, ignoring his pleas. She had seen people, who in better times had been friends of her mother, look away when they met her, afraid of being accused of forbidden talking, or even knowing the wife of a Cambodian soldier if authorities found out. Chanbopha watched this change in grownups. It left her frightened and very alone not understanding this new world.

One night a woman appeared at their door begging for food. Ma had been preparing mice she had caught and smuggled in from the rice fields, cutting off their heads, feet and tails before popping them into the soup simmering on the small fire.

Chan recognized the woman as someone much talked about for her wealth in Phnom Penh. Ma had pointed her out on one of their Sunday outings as her gleaming limousine passed. "She never walks but is driven by her chauffeur for even the shortest distance. It's said she even calls a maid to pick up her handkerchief if she drops it." Ma's voice quivered with disapproval but Chan had admired the woman's intricate hair-do and thought her vibrant makeup glamorous. Right then she decided to be like her someday.

That one vision had become her ideal and she had looked for similar photos in Ma's paper, cutting them out and hiding them under her pillow.

Now here was that same fine lady, emaciated and filthy, her hair stringy and wearing the same black as everyone else. "Please, I am so hungry." She looked longingly at the discarded mouse entrails and remnants on the table.

"But you can't eat that and I don't have enough food for my own family," said Ma.

Chan quietly gathered the mouse pieces in her hands and took them to the woman who grasped them like treasure and disappeared into the night.

Ma looked reprovingly at her daughter, then shrugged and sighed, but said nothing.

The woman appeared often after that and Chan began to save some meatier pieces of whatever they had to add to the entrails she gave away. Ma pretended not to notice and although the former socialite never said thank you Chan felt better for it.

After a month or so the woman stopped coming and for a while Chan saved the bits of mice; then they began to smell and she threw them away.

CHAPTER TWELVE

Ma was needing more of the food, to feed the baby inside her, she said.

Afraid of getting caught if she smuggled larger portions from the kitchen Chanbopha cut her own rations and by day's end in the rice paddies was often ready to collapse from hunger. Getting through her kitchen duties was a matter of will power, always anxious that the women would not want her there if she didn't manage to do everything they asked.

It was a June afternoon when she discovered a solution.

The rice was being harvested and Chan walked beside one of the slow moving oxen as it pulled a laden cart. The sun was fierce. She itched and ached and hurt all over. Looking down at the ground, as the animal's hooves crunched over green cuttings spilled from previous journeys, Chan's eyes focused on rice grains being forced out and crushed. Quickly she scooped some up and stuffed them into her mouth. How good to have something to chew. She swallowed and bent for more. This was real rice even if it wasn't cooked—and her stomach welcomed it.

From then on, each day during harvesting she walked beside the wagon, sneaking crushed brown rice kernels into her mouth, restoring her strength while creating a legacy of damaged teeth.

The days wore on: picking up cow dung in the morning, break for soup then out to the rice fields and later back to the kitchen. Everyone had lost track of the days and months. Only the ends and beginnings of the monsoon rains informed of season changes and, although first downpours were a relief, soon being constantly wet, slogging through mud and being bitten by the clouds of mosquitoes became miserable. People died of fevers and the guards grumbled to themselves and frequently flew into rages.

One morning Chan noticed that a water buffalo had calved during the night. The rain stopped and the sun drew steam like a delicate curtain around the two as she worked her way close. The new mother made no objection as Chan approached her baby and as the fawn colored calf lifted her muzzle toward its first human Chan scratched the hard little forehead and looked into the soft eyes. "Somewhere there must still be good people." She whispered into the calf's big ear. "You remind me that there is beauty. For a while, some months back I saw it then I forgot to look."

'Hey! Are you working?" a guard shouted.

As she bent to pick up more dung Chanbopha resolved that instead of hearing the hated orders and threats she would listen to the birds singing in the Guava branches. When she carried Srey out each morning she would look for sunlight limning trees in the darkest jungle and she would hear the music of insects but ignore their sting. She would look again for the colorful parrot and cheeky monkeys and laugh at their antics.

From that day Chan used her imagination to escape from her sordid surroundings. Sometimes she sang, quietly, songs she had learned in that almost forgotten big room where Ma and her tutor had taught her lessons. Everyone assumed her brain had been affected by fever as had happened to many, so when she looked overlong at a flower or smiled at the sky they ignored it. Besides people were too busy with their own troubles to notice others. There was starvation and dysentery which even the stolen, boiled skin of the guava tree failed to cure; also beriberi, malaria and a few suspected cases of cholera. All that, apart from the broken bones which couldn't be fixed, injured eyes, cuts and skin eruptions kept everyone too busy to care how one child behaved.

The smells were bad all over camp but Chan would try to replace them with the remembered scent of roses her mother had long ago brought to the apartment. As she ran between the rows of huts, seeing bodies carried out, she would think of the sweet calf and run on. Familiar faces disappeared overnight but that was now the norm. One thing she could not ignore was the obvious fact that Ma's time was close.

CHAPTER THIRTEEN

It came on the night of a full moon. "Chan, Chan—wake up!"

Chan immediately knew what it was and jumped out of bed, eyes still half closed. "Yes, Ma. I'll fetch Uncle."

"Be careful!"

All known doctors in the camp had been killed by the Pol Pot and as a result many women had died in childbirth made more perilous due to malnutrition and overwork. But Ma knew that an Uncle who lived halfway down the village had been a doctor in Phnom Penh. Only by acting the part of the uneducated laborer had he survived. Now Chanbopha ran as fast as she could, darting from one shadow to another, shadows made blacker by the full moon. Soon she was on the way back with Uncle close behind. He immediately went to Ma sending the rest of them running to get water, light a fire in the tin can, and bring something to wrap the baby in. Chanbopha stayed to soothe Srey who shivered at the far corner of the big bed frightened by the sounds of her mother's labor. "It's here," whispered Uncle. "A girl."

But there was only the weakest mewl from the undersized infant and Chan cringed from sight of its frailty.

Uncle wrapped the baby in an old sack Chan had smuggled from the kitchen. "She will need milk but I don't think your mother has any. See how empty she is. You must try to give the baby soup. I know that is all you have. Is there something hot for your Ma now? She needs strength."

Chan ran to get the cup left from earlier. It contained a valuable piece of chicken she had hoped to save for herself. Now she was grateful she had it to give to Ma who drifted off to sleep, the baby at her empty breast.

Uncle slipped back into the night. After a moment there was a burst of gunfire, a scream, and the excited chatter of guards. Then quiet. It was a common occurrence and most weary prisoners now slept through such interruptions. Chan told herself it was only bored guards shooting at rats. But tonight a chill ran through her. They never saw Uncle again.

Chanbopha slept. The baby awoke her with tremulous wails and she lay fretting about how to feed it. Then the answer came and, finding a bottle, she crept into the last of that night and padded down the path to the field she knew only too well. It didn't take long to find the cow and calf she had befriended and the sleepy mother allowed herself to be milked so the bottle was almost full before the calf pushed in for his share.

"Thank you, Mother," Chanbopha whispered and ran as quickly as possible without spilling back to the camp.

"Look, I have milk!" she whispered as she entered their hut.

She ripped a piece off her shirt, which was little more than a rag anyway, twisted it and soaked it in the still warm milk. Then she put it to the infant's mouth. The hungry little creature sucked with gusto consuming most of what Chan had collected, before relaxing into a peaceful sleep.

Chan was asleep almost as soon but this time with the joy of her mother's gratitude in her ears.

Finding food took up all Chanbopha's spare moments. Apart from getting milk for the baby, named Cass, every grub and insect, leaf or root, rodent or snail, had potential for nourishment when added to the two times a day collection of soup. Baby Cass had soup added to her diet of milk but was always hungry and seemed to shrink rather than grow. The kitchen workers, missing their own families, lavished chicken leftovers from the guards' meals on Chan, obviously enjoying her effusive thanks. Chan learned how to manipulate those women, playing one against another into giving more while she hid most of it in the pouch tucked under her shirt. Even so the food, divided among five, still needed a lot added to it

Ma was soon working in the fields again with her new baby tied to her back. One night when Chanbopha returned from milking the cow, tiny Cass would not take hold of the wad of milk-dripping shirt. "Take it!" Chan hissed trying to force it between unresponsive lips. She poured milk from the cup into the baby's mouth but it ran out the other side. Too weary to cry Chan put the milk down and fell asleep.

She awoke to Ma's wail. Cass was a cold lifeless bundle being rocked in her mother's arms while the two boys tried to console her.

They washed the tiny corpse then, under a full moon, the four of them, Srey even now refusing to set foot on the ground, went weeping into the jungle. Vuthy led the way carrying the almost weightless body and it was he who dug a grave with his hands in the soft loam at the foot of an ancient tree. Carefully he laid one month old Cass in it and covered her with soil.

Soon she will be just another piece of the jungle, thought Chan. Poor little thing never had a chance to be a real person. But perhaps her next reincarnation will be in a better place. Maybe she's lucky to miss this one.

To the soft sound of Ma's prayers the guilt Chan had been harboring over her secret relief at no longer having to brave dark nights to milk the cow and find more food faded and disappeared.

Ma didn't regain full strength for many months after Cass' birth and death. The family was always hungry but better off than most people around them. Sometimes they would talk about meals they had eaten in Phnom Penh and what they dreamed of someday having again.

Chanbopha was thinking of that one evening as she followed Ma into the jungle and began their nightly search. Her pleasure at finding a cluster of mushrooms was interrupted by Ma's voice calling and she ran to see what she had found.

Her mother was on her hands and knees peering into a large hole. "Something big to fill our pot tonight." she whispered.

""What is it?" asked Chanbopha kneeling beside her. "The hole is very big."

Ma smiled. "Very delicious." She said. "See if you can find another end. We can't let whatever it is escape."

It was a long time since Ma had smiled and Chan didn't want to spoil the moment with misgivings so she searched for, and found, an opening which matched the first. "It's here," she whispered as loud as she dared.

Ma called back, voice quivering with excitement. "Get a stick and poke the rat or whatever it is out this way. My knife is ready."

Chan ripped off a half dead palm frond and stuffed it down the hole. It met resistance then was released and moved farther in.

All of a sudden there was the sound of struggle and Ma shrieked. Chan ran, stumbling and falling in the darkness. She arrived to find her mother battling something big and strong. It was a moment before she made out the huge writhing serpent. Chan didn't know how to help. Its great coils wrapped around Ma, its tail thrashing, tongue darting as Ma desperately stabbed with her one weapon which seemed puny against such power. Chan watched, impotent, horrified, expecting to see Ma's life squeezed out of her. But it was the snake which crumpled and collapsed.

By sheer luck the knife had reached a vital spot. Ma shook herself loose. She looked elated and strong for the first time since they'd left Phnom Penh. "Many good meals," she said. "We must get him back to camp."

The serpent was heavy and Ma took its head while Chan draped the tail over her shoulder. As they walked Chan wondered at how she had no qualms touching this creature which not so long ago would have sent her running in the opposite direction. And how proud she was of Ma for killing it! She would never have imagined her mother capable of such bravery. Hunger won over fear and right now everything edible was life—never taste nor smell anymore- just sustenance.

They bore their trophy triumphantly into their hut where Sovirak and Vuthy crowded around and helped stretch the long body out while Chanbopha told the story of its capture. Vuthy said it was a Golden tree snake. Ma brandished her knife and raised it to cut enough chops for several meals. Even Srey sat up to see what was happening. There had never been such excitement in the hut since they'd arrived.

"What is this? What do you have there?' Two guards burst in.

Vuthy stepped in front of them. "This is ours. We caught it. We need it for strength to work for Pol Pot." Sovirak joined in pleading while Chan held Ma back from trying to intervene.

For these two bored guards taking this luscious meal almost from the mouths of the starving was only sport so, after baiting the boys a few minutes longer, they hoisted the snake into their arms and left, laughing.

Ma and the two boys stood watching them go, shoulders slumped.

"Look!" Chanbopha's high treble made heads jerk up and eyes fix on the small figure standing, smiling, in front of them. Their eyes travelled on to the red meat she held high above her head and then they all smiled. Chan had cut chunks from the choicest part of the snake while everyone else was arguing. After the hugging and congratulating had subsided, the meat was cooked over the little fire behind the house and soon they were all devouring succulent steaks. Even Srey chewed a small piece. The Oum family slept well that night.

CHAPTER FOURTEEN

Days dragged on. Insects continued to bite, sores and bouts of dysentery took their turns, torn muscles and work injuries had to be ignored. Ma's spirits seemed better for a few days after the night of the snake then she went back to feeling poorly again.

A week later, Srey died.

No one really noticed that the child hadn't spoken for days and when Chanbopha carried her out to the jungle to relieve herself she was as light as a wisp of smoke. One day when Ma returned from work she found her child crumpled on the ground beside the bed. Dead she was little different than when she'd been alive and although Chanbopha grieved for her little sister she did not feel anything for the emaciated corpse.

Again Vuthy carried a dead child out after dark and they wept as he buried her close to where Ma's baby lay. Chan almost shouted for them to stop when they shoveled soil over her. It didn't seem fair that little Srey who died from her fear of touching dirt must now be enveloped in it.

Sometimes Chanbopha tried to remember how life had been before the Khmer Rouge, but every day it seemed to fade farther away. Reality was now: this prison filled with fear and pain and hopelessness. This place where she had the responsibility of an adult although she was only a child. She watched butterflies flutter like brilliant flowers through the long grass then fly high, away from the fetid smells and brutality below. She watched until they disappeared, and longed to join them. Sometimes in dreams she did and looked down on a world where children played on swings and laughed and mothers and fathers danced together and took families out to dinners. Chan realized she'd almost forgotten what having a full stomach was like and could barely remember her father's face. That chilled her. What if she didn't know him when he arrived to take her away from here! What if he didn't recognize her and took some other little girl! After all he hadn't seen her since she was five and that was three years ago. She had grown.

Another calf was born to Chan's special water buffalo cow and sometimes after work in the hot kitchen she would sneak off to the field and sit in moonlight watching them graze, soothed by their deep, soft breaths.

That's where she'd been on the evening Vuthy didn't return from work. They waited, saved his soup until ants found it and invaded the hut, biting them in their beds. No one could sleep as they waited for his footsteps which never came. They knew he was dead but no one could say it. Chanbopha was numb. It was as though part of her inner strength was ripped away. She remembered how kind Vuthy had been. How when she was small and no one would play with her, he would. He had been like a second father although he was so young. The pain in her heart seemed too big to bear.

For five days misery weighed on Chan then one night on her way home from the kitchen a man stepped out from the shadows. She drew in a startled breath then recognized him as someone she often met in the soup line and whose smile told her he knew her ploy of going through more than once.

"I have a message," he whispered. "About your brother Vuthy. He and my son were moved to another work camp. That's all I know, but they are alive," For a moment his eyes caught hers and she knew it was true. Then the man was gone and she stood alone in the middle of the path.

Such joy! She looked up at the stars, thanking them and, forgetting tiredness, ran home to tell the others,

They would miss him terribly- but Vuthy was alive!

Monsoon rains returned and the Oums sat inside watching the compound turn into a lake and shrinking away from drips that came through the thatch. They still had to go to their work in the fields unless it was a really bad storm with thunder and lightning-then nobody left shelter even to go for their soup ration. The tumult frightened Chan and Ma drew her and Sovirak onto the bed beside her and talked about things barely remembered, like games played with forgotten friends.

"Will we see good times again, Ma?" Chan asked.

"Of course," Ma answered. "Fighting will end and then we can go home. Now let's do some lessons. A little French, maybe."

Later, when the storm hushed they prayed in front of the small shrine Ma had set up in the corner—but the Buddha Chan prayed to wore an army uniform and promised he'd be home from America soon.

The older relatives they knew in the camp had disappeared. Even the grandmother who used to help with little Srey was gone.

The ladies in the kitchen yawned a lot, smoked more and paid little attention to Chan, taking all the work she did for granted. They also didn't notice or care how much she took home with her so the three Oums ate well.

The guards also had relaxed and played cards instead of harassing workers. The atmosphere of the camp had changed.

CHAPTER FIFTEEN

Vuthy had been gone a year. Then one night there he was, walking through their door. It was dark and at first they were frightened at the arrival of this strange man.

"Vuthy!" Ma was first to recognize him.

Chanbopha, disbelieving, stayed frozen in place. Then she ran and jumped into his arms squealing, "Vuthy! Vuthy!"

Soon the three of them were hugging and crying.

Sovirak woke up and joined them. "You are so thin!" he said feeling his adopted brother's ribs, "But you are taller."

And he was; the year of hard work had changed Vuthy into a man. "Where have you been?" Ma asked.

"Working in the jungle. Every day clearing more. We got better food there though. But I wanted to get back to you so when I saw my chance I escaped."

The guards didn't seem to notice his return and Chan figured all the prisoners looked alike now, skinny, ragged and dirty. She had long ago decided the reason Communists wanted everyone to have short hair was because they all had lice like she and her family did now.

Vuthy told them of rumors in the other camp that Vietnam was about to attack Cambodia and drive out the Pol Pot. "When that happens we will be free!" he said. Ma seemed to get a whole new lease on life after hearing that and began school lessons at night for Chan and Sovirak although they were all so tired it was hard to stay awake. Now Chan awoke each morning wondering if this day would be the one.

It was late 1979 and talk among the kitchen workers had an excited streak running through it. Instead of working they stood around chattering in sharp, frightened voices. Chan tried to understand why things were different but apart from a pervading sense of distraction among all the camp's Pol Pot soldiers, each day continued as usual.

"What is it? What is happening?" Chan asked Vuthy, who seemed able to answer questions better than anyone else.

"I think we will soon be free," he said.

She thought about that as she worked among the rice stalks that afternoon and wondered what being free really meant. Freedom was said to be a wonderful thing but what would they do with it!

Then one morning, when her group was collecting dung in the pasture someone noticed their guard was gone. They worked on, keeping one eye on the place where he should reappear. But he didn't. Tentatively the children filed back to camp.

Chan trotted straight to the kitchen. It was deserted. Vegetables wilted in their baskets and soup congealed on the cool stove. Flies buzzed over meat on the cutting board.

Chanbopha ran to their hut but it was empty. She waited inside, hearing faint movements from neighbors but seeing no one. A parrot's squawk broke the ghostly quiet. Ma came through the door and Chan ran to her. "What is happening? The kitchen is empty. Everyone is gone!"

Ma put her finger over her daughter's mouth, "Shh, maybe good things. Be still and wait."

Vuthy and Sovirak arrived full of questions but no answers.

They waited and waited. No sounds came from outside. Not even a bird's call or monkey's chatter. Chanbopha, unable to stand it any longer, peeked out. Nothing. Not one soldier hovered in the barren yard. Faces peered from other huts and finally one man stepped outside. Then others. Ma came to look over Chan's shoulder. Where were the usual angry shouts of guards? Nothing. Slowly people emerged, muttering their confusion.

An engine's roar shattered the silence and a truck plunged through the main gate. It jolted to a stop and a soldier in a khaki uniform sprang out. He held a megaphone to his lips. "Attention Cambodian prisoners. We of the Vietnamese Army release you from the tyranny of the Khmer Rouge. You are now free to go back to your homes."

Someone gave a small cheer then all the people swarmed from their huts. After a few minutes many went back inside.

"What do we do, Ma?" Chan said." Can we go home?"

"Vuthy, what do we do now?" asked Ma.

Vuthy, stood tall as befit the man of the family. "We can't go home. I told you about the cousin who came through that different camp I was in, well he informed me that others have taken our apartment in Phnom Penh. It is theirs now. We must go north and make a new life."

Outside, people were leaving, weak and shuffling but driven to depart at their first opportunity. It was hard to tell men from women, old from young, all emaciated and clothed in black rags.

Night was close. "We will rest and leave at dawn. Sleep everyone, we have a long walk tomorrow." Ma pulled Chan inside just as a girl Chan had worked next to in the dung field limped by. They had never spoken but this time each gave the other a small wave.

Chan did sleep and awoke to a strangely quiet new day. The bed beside her was empty and she knew Ma was saying goodbye to the two daughters she must leave buried under the big tree she would never see again. When she returned she said nothing and her eyes were red.

"Eat something, Ma." Chan gently guided her mother to the edge of their bed where they always sat to eat, and the four of them finished everything they had, mostly leavings Chan had brought from the kitchen. Then, carrying nothing but their plastic cups, the bundle of clothes they had arrived in four years before, and some coins Ma had kept hidden, they headed for freedom.

A body lay just outside the gate. Chan recognized it as the young guard who had taken them to the field each day. He, who had harassed and beaten them, always thinking up ways to make their lives more miserable, now lay like a rag doll—his face as innocent as a child's.

CHAPTER SIXTEEN

It was strange to be able to make choices—to have to make them. Most of the people turned south toward Phnom Penh.

"No," Vuthy stopped Ma who had begun to follow them. "Phnom Penh will be in turmoil. There is nothing that way for us."

Ma's shoulders sank and for a moment she stood looking after the flood of those heading South, then her chin lifted and she turned to face the opposite direction. "Then we must go this way," she said and began plodding up the road.

Just four of us now, thought Chanbopha. But what about Papa? She tugged on Vuthy's elbow. "But Papa?" She wanted to say more but panic choked her so no words got through. Sovirak stopped and looked back the other way.

Vuthy spoke quickly, in the man's voice he had lately acquired. "We must go to the refugee camp over the Thai border. It's called, Khao-I-Dang and is the best.

Not as dangerous as some. Papa will look for us there. I know—I was told that."

For a moment they looked at him, then they believed and trudged on, catching up to Ma.

"It's a long way," she said.

"We'll stop at the first village and stay for a while. Find work," said Vuthy. "Surely people will want to help us."

But people didn't. They turned their backs on the four skeletal creatures in their ragged Khmer Rouge clothes. When they asked for a place to stay they were hustled on their way;

told the village was already too full, with too many mouths to feed. Ma offered one of her precious coins for some noodles but the woman laughed. "Riels are useless. Don't you know that? Communism is all barter. No more money!"

"But Pol Pot is finished! Surely everything will go back to how it was." Ma tried to remonstrate.

"They are ignorant villagers who know nothing of that," said Vuthy. "Let's go."

So they walked on, sleeping in fields near the road, huddled together for warmth and comfort. Chanbopha had stolen a loaf of bread while they were being chivied from the last village and now Ma scolded half heartedly with her mouth stuffed full.

Sometimes Chanbopha almost wished herself back in the prison camp where at least they had their own familiar bed and knew where to get food. She had dreamed of the outside world as a good place with friends, where everything would be as it once was—and Papa would be there. But it wasn't that way at all.

And so they moved on as 'New People,' facing rejection from the 'Old People' of every village.

Chan's feet hurt in her tire tread sandals and she hardly bothered to look up from the road. At first she had been angry at the people who were rude to her mother and ordered them to leave a village, now she expected nothing else. Not a word passed between the four of them as they struggled along what seemed endless miles.

"Oh!"

They all stopped and looked at Ma whose face had brightened as she stared at a post with the name of the next village on it.

"I know this place. I have a cousin here. We played together as children." Ma took Chan's hand and broke into a quicker shuffle.

Villagers met them with the usual coldness but when Ma mentioned the name of her relative frowns changed to smiles and they were escorted down the main street to a wooden house on its own at the far end. A small woman, scrawny and malnourished, like one of those chickens which are forever pecking, came blinking to the door.

After a few moments of suspicious staring she let out a cry of recognition then pulled Ma inside, the others following. She waved them toward the few shaky chairs and kept talking while she made tea. It was exciting for both her and Ma as they recalled old and better times. The Oums pulled out their own cups, guessing this new auntie may not have enough, and Chan was happy to bury her face in the steam of the slightly tea colored hot water poured into hers. "Of course you can stay here, lots of room with only me and my children," the woman shrilled. "And the boys can help repair the roof that leaks so badly—and dig the garden." Auntie went outside and Chan heard a chicken squawking, then a few minutes later saw it, newly naked, carried into the kitchen and plunged into a pot of boiling water. Vegetables were dropped in afterward. Vuthy and Sovirak brought rainwater from the cistern and Ma helped Chan wash herself all over, including her hair. It was like a dream to be clean and in a real house.

Chan was so sleepy she stumbled upstairs and collapsed onto the bed she was to share with Ma. Lulled by the distant voices of the two women, she slept.

It was almost dark when Auntie called her down for bowls of rich chicken soup and rice. They ate quickly then the boys threw mats on the floor of the front room and said goodnight. Chanbopha sighed as she went back upstairs, her tummy full, and unafraid for the first time in a long while.

Next morning Chan dug into the bundle they had carried with them and found her old yellow shorts and top, still grubby from the long walk from Phnom Penh, but at least not Khmer Rouge black. They went on easily, baggier and looser than before but she was surprised to find a large gap between top and shorts, leaving her midriff bare. She knew she was all bones, everyone was, but hadn't realized her added height. After all she must be ten now. Birthdays had gone unnoticed when no one knew the current date anyway.

Eager to explore the village, Chan slipped outside. People were already busy; men leading oxen to the fields, children lugging full buckets from the nearby river and women sweeping their door stoops. Chickens strutted and scratched while roosters crowed and goats nibbled whatever they could find. A large sow grunted as she rootled in a nearby ditch. Chan appreciated the villager's colorful clothes and she pledged to never wear black again. The faces she saw were plumper than any she had seen in a long time and these people certainly weren't afraid to talk. Chan thought this as their shrill voices and laughter cut through the warm air and it brought back memories of the busy streets of Phnom Penh. But these were not her people. She wanted Papa and everything to be as it was. She hungered to be where people knew how to read and talked about more than farming; were polite and clean, with indoor plumbing.

She ran back to the house where her sleepy eyed Ma, Sovirak, Vuthy, Auntie and her three sulky looking teenage sons were all having tea and rice. She settled, crosslegged beside them, eating while the others planned their future.

"I need to make a business," said Ma. "Coming through the other, inhospitable villages on our way here I noticed how many people seemed cold, shivering under meager wraps. I used to be good with the needles and knit shawls for my mother and family. If I can find wool perhaps I can make some and use them to trade."

"I know just the woman!" Auntie interrupted. "Mrs. Wu, at the other end of the village has goats. She combs their heavy coats then makes it into coarse wool. She'll sell cheap. Maybe exchange for boys' work."

Everyone was talking at once, and Chanbopha, swept up in the excitement, scampered ahead as ten minutes later they headed up the street towards Mrs. Wu's. While the adults haggled and inspected yarn Chan was being inspected and accepted by Mrs. Wu's two children who were about her age.

They took her outside to show off some baby chicks and then they chased each other, running around the house. To play again! And shout! And laugh! Chan couldn't believe it was happening! When Ma called she arrived flushed and panting and her mother looked at her, smiling, "Good, you have friends. You will have lots of time to play. Now you must help Auntie and me carry this yarn home."

From then on Auntie's house was abuzz with activity. Ma taught her friend to knit so the two of them spent hours creating shawls while Chanbopha wound the yarn and cooked the meals. Vuthy and Sovirak were down at the wool seller's working off the trade but Chan never did know what Auntie's sons did during the day. They only seemed to come home to eat and probably sleep. Everyone was tired at night and the living room was filling up with shawls while people in the village were beginning to show interest.

CHAPTER SEVENTEEN

Chan learned to play with other children and even attended the village school, which was frustrating as she knew more than the teacher and none of the other students could yet read nor seemed to care.

Sometimes, at night, she worried that she wasn't any closer to finding her father. Surely they weren't going to stay in this village forever!

Ma worked hard but in exchange for rent Auntie had Ma barter most of the shawls for rice which was then traded for other food. Each day she recited a long list of groceries for Ma to get but Chan saw few of the luxury items on their table—always the same chicken soup, rice, and vegetables from the garden.

She hadn't noticed the disintegration of Ma and Auntie's friendship until the day when she came home after school and heard them screaming at each other. Auntie demanded more rent. "It is inconvenient and costly having so many people in this small house. I deserve chocolates from the market and good things, maybe a new sarong."

Chan crept to her bedroom and after a short time Ma burst in.

"Gather your things. Tomorrow we leave this place where we are not wanted."

Ma left to tell the boys and Chan looked around the room, seeing how little she had to take. At least the few clothes and shoes she did have were better and newer than the ones she had arrived with two months earlier.

Chanbopha, her two brothers and Ma left very early and each had a bag of yarn to carry with their own trappings. They also had a little food Ma had hidden and a bundle of shawls to trade. Any twinge of regret Chanbopha felt at leaving the friends she had made was soon forgotten in her relief at setting out again to find Papa.

The Auntie she had liked less each day had not appeared to see them off but Chan did wave once when she looked back and thought she saw a shadow in the window.

Now they looked more respectable someone from the village soon picked them up in his ancient truck. He dropped them off at the next village but Ma took one look at the scattering of humble houses and grunted. "No good for our business here, we must go farther."

They started walking and were again given rides: and so they covered country miles by ox-cart and car. Once they were jammed onto a motorcycle and sidecar. Every time buildings appeared in the distance Chanbopha perked up, then was disappointed. She was hot and tired. "Why couldn't we stay in that village?" she grumbled.

"Because it's too small," snapped Ma. "Hurry, we must get there before dark."

But where was 'there'? Chan dragged her feet. The boys had long ago gone quiet and even though Vuthy had talked Chan into letting him carry her bag of yarn, the rest of her few belongings weighed more every moment. She had to fight off tears and part of it was her shame at showing weakness. She had always prided herself on being the strong one. She prayed the next vehicle would provide a ride. And finally one did.

"This looks better!" Ma's shout awoke Chan from the doze she had fallen into in spite of the jolting of the wagon. They had been offered the chance to ride on top of knobbly sacks containing some kind of root vegetables, and without hesitation climbed aboard. Two bay horses, zebra striped with sweat, pulled them along and the clip clop of their hooves had been a lullaby. Now Chan and the boys raised themselves to look ahead through the gathering dusk and Chan's heart rose like a sunburst in her throat. Lights! A city. A real city!

It certainly was more of a city than the villages they had seen the past few days but if Chan expected even a smaller Phnom Penh she was sorely disappointed. However Ma took one look at the bustling main street and said. "This is where we will stay."

They left the wagon and started up a side road where the farmer who had provided their last lift said they could find cheap accommodation. Chanbopha didn't care where they went as long as she could sleep, and barely noticed the small shabby room with two beds onto which the four of them collapsed to remain unconscious until morning. There was no running water and only a ditch out back for a toilet. As she used it Chan thought how accustomed she had become to things that would have horrified her back in the days she thought of as real life.

Ma had already been out and burst in with a summons. "Come everyone! I have breakfast."

Chan couldn't believe her nose and eyes. Fresh rolls tumbled out of the bag to be followed by a can of condensed milk and a bottle of water.

They were soon sitting at the scarred table dipping rolls into the mix of warm sweet milk and water. If Chan closed her eyes she could imagine Papa sitting up there at the head of his family just as he used to when they ate this favorite breakfast almost every morning.

Ma spoke. "We must quickly find a place to live where I can knit my shawls. Chanbopha, you will sell them when they are done and, boys, you must get work. Now, everyone, off to find our new home"

"I'll find somewhere," said Vuthy.

"I will be first," said Sovirak.

Out in the lane Chanbopha watched her brothers split off in different directions and felt a resurgence of her old competitive spirit. She turned and hurried toward the main thoroughfare. Here she dodged in and out between people who seemed well fed and too busy to notice her.

CHAPTER EIGHTEEN

Although much bigger than any town they had seen lately this one was really quite small and Chan soon left the main shopping area and was among narrow alleys lined by old, leaning buildings which appeared to be apartments. Women chatted and children played. One grandmother hunkered outside a door smoking a pipe.

"Hello, Child," she called to Chan. "I have not seen you before."

Chan went over. "My mother and two brothers just came to town last night. We need somewhere to live."

The old woman peered at her through rheumy eyes. "You look very thin. Where is your father?"

"He is in the army, Auntie, an officer, but in America, otherwise he would have saved us from the Khmer Rouge." She stopped. She could be killed for telling that secret! How had she forgotten? But the old woman seemed not to notice.

"You were in one of those prison camps they put city folks in?"

Was that good or bad? Was she supposed to be educated or not? After those tight lipped four years Chan didn't know enemy from friend. "We need somewhere to live. Ma has money and a job." This was stretching it a bit but the old woman's eyes lit up.

She struggled to her feet and began to hobble down the lane. "Follow me, Child. My daughter has a place perhaps."

Chan squeezed her nostrils tight and told herself she could get used to the smell of sewage if only they had a place of their own that was dry and warm. Then they could all work and save to travel to the border and that refugee camp Vuthy had told them about. She had heard of it again another day while peeling vegetables in the prison kitchen. The cooks were chattering among themselves about relatives who had gone to such a place and then been allowed to join kin in some far off country. For the first time Chan had realized two things: one was that the cooks in the prison camp kitchen had also been prisoners wanting to be somewhere else and second that being legally classified as a refugee was the key to getting out of the Khmer Rouge clutches. And reaching Papa.

They had gone through a rickety gate into a small dusty yard. The old woman screeched a name and soon a very pregnant girl appeared with a basket of laundry on her hip. The old woman spoke in a Khmer dialect Chanbopha could barely understand then the young woman ran inside. From the sounds Chan guessed she was making the place presentable. Perhaps she herself was living there. After ten minutes of waiting the young woman reappeared and with a toothless smile ushered them in. Two of the three small ground floor rooms were dimly lit by narrow slits but the third had larger windows and the door through which, when open, good daylight flooded. Ma could work here.

"How much and what can we trade for this?" Chanbopha asked.

"Trade? We exchange riel here, Child." The old woman cackled. "That Pol Pot nonsense went when they did. If your Ma has no money..." She shrugged and began to turn away.

Chan's heart sank then she brightened, remembering the small sack Ma had kept buried in a corner of their hut. "But she has!" she blurted praying it was so. "I'll be back soon!"

Chan set off at a run to find Ma, all the while praying that the money was there and that the boys' searches had been unsuccessful. After several false turns she recognized the street she sought and her face broke into a grin as she saw the disconsolate expressions on her family's faces.

Ma sat on a nearby step. "Well, what did you find? I found nothing. Either dangerous neighborhood, too expensive, too small or too dark. I hope one of you did better."

Both boys shook their heads and looked at the ground. Chan suspected they had spent the time exploring the town and looking at pretty girls.

Ma heaved a great sigh. "Well we must find some place." She stood up and faced back down the street.

"You didn't ask me," said Chanbopha, loudly enough to have everyone turn startled eyes on her.

"We didn't expect you to find anything," said Sovirak with the condescension of a slightly older brother.

"Well, I did. Ma, do you have money? They are using that again here."

Ma nodded.

"Good! Then we can move right in." Chan let out a sigh of relief, and couldn't help giving Sovirak a 'so there' sniff and lift of her chin.

They all went inside, collected their belongings, and gathered in the street.

"Let's go," said Chan.

Vuthy shrugged, "Might as well."

And the three of them followed Chan back to the narrow street she had recently left.

The old woman met them and took them to the apartment which Ma quickly accepted and, after handing over some carefully counted coins, the Oum family moved in. As the door closed behind them there were three sighs of relief to have a 'home' again but Chan gave a sigh of pride knowing she was the hero of the day.

Ma quickly got to work making shawls. The boys took on odd jobs, whatever needed a strong back, and Chan was sent to find the town market and best place to set up her booth. Throughout the following days she came to know the streets and which vendors would not try to cheat her because she was a child but would give her extra when she bought something. She cooked the meals so Ma could keep working and when there were enough shawls she took them to the market and her voice could be heard loud and clear among others touting their wares. The shawls were popular and she sold them for more than Ma said and hid the extra away for when they would go to find Papa. That, as always, was her goal. It stopped her from envying the children she saw going to school each morning, and from hating the bad smells that seeped in through their doors and windows. She did however resent the fact that, because she could buy no new clothes, people saw her as a peasant child and not the literate officer's daughter she was.

It was two years since they'd been freed from the Pol Pot camp. Chanbopha was twelve and her hair was long again and tied in two sleek bunches. These she stroked as she daydreamed late in an afternoon, resting her voice which was hoarse from trying to sell the last shawl in front of her. A woman stopped. She looked familiar; someone from the distant past. "How much are you asking, Child?"

The gravelly voice brought back a scene of women hovering over the radio in their old apartment in Phnom Penh. "Auntie Thuy?"

The woman looked startled. "Who are you?"

"Chanbopha. Don't you remember me? Chanbopha Oum."

"Little Chan! You have grown! We thought you were dead. Where is your Ma?"

"Come. I will take you. She will be so happy." Chan rolled up the unsold shawl and led their way through the dwindling market crowd. From glances at her companion Chan saw that she didn't look as poor and thin as those who had been incarcerated. She wondered how she had escaped that, but knew it was a question best not asked.

Ma was thrilled to see her old friend, and Chan prepared supper as the women talked.

She almost dropped one of their few plates when she heard Auntie say, "I almost forgot. I saw Ssu the other day. She is moving to a refugee camp across the Thai border. She asked about you. Said she had word of your husband. He was looking for you."

Chan ran to Ma, not caring that she interrupted. "Where is she? Oh Ma, Pa is coming for us. Oh Ma, we must find this woman."

Ma sat unable to speak.

Chan whirled to the Auntie, gripping her arm. "Please, where is she? Please, we must find this woman now."

"Patience, Child!" said Auntie Thuy.

"Yes, please do take us to her!" Ma began to push Thuy toward the door. Chanbopha grabbed the tail of the Auntie's shirt and was jumping up and down shouting, "Papa, Papa! He will take us to America!"

"Stop!" Auntie Thuy said. "This was a long time ago. Everyone thought you were dead. Besides you need money to get into a refugee camp. Many riels. First the camp, then the visa."

Ma put a restraining hand on Chan's shoulder. "How much?"

"More than you can make in many years of selling shawls."

"Is camp better than here?"

"They have water… and decent food. Ssu tells me they also teach English there so when your relative sends money for the trip you are ready."

"Can we go Ma? Please?" Chan pleaded.

" We don't have enough Riel, you know that."

Chan turned back to Auntie. "Why don't you go if it's better than here?"

"Because I have no one in America to sponsor me. Always problems for us these days. Now I must go home. If I see Ssu I will tell her I saw you."

And she was gone leaving Ma and Chan staring after her. Chan felt as though her heart had been torn out of her and thrown away. Papa had been looking for them but they could not reach him nor tell him they were alive. Money was either a bridge to, or a wall against, getting things in this life. The

Khmer Rouge destroyed the Bank and would have killed them for having the forbidden currency but now, without it, they were unable to reach Papa. She took the coins she had earned that day from her pocket. Barely enough to feed them all and pay rent. The boys would bring some home from odd jobs but it would take a long time to have enough. She hadn't even asked how much. Having to pay to get into the refugee camp had never crossed her mind. Chan was so filled with sorrow she thought she would drown.

She could barely eat the rice and chicken she had made and she knew her mother felt just as miserable because she came straight to bed instead of weaving shawls late as she usually did. Chan's mind was in a turmoil. She had to do something. There must be a solution!

CHAPTER NINETEEN

Chan awoke early and quickly dressed, slipping quietly out into the street intent on finding the auntie who had brought the news of Papa. Having him to sponsor their way to America was evidently one of the two tickets enabling entrance to the refugee camp. Surely, having one, she could manage the money part somehow. If only she could find Auntie Thuy and get information on how to find her friend.

Chan trotted along alleys empty but for the odd scrawny dog, and fatter cats due to there being more rats than food scraps to be found. She was relieved to reach the market place where she spent so many hours selling Ma's beautiful shawls. But of course the square was empty. What next? Had she really expected Auntie Thuy to be here at this hour? She must live nearby, her stoutness suggested that she wouldn't walk far from where she lived, also that she had been eating well and was living alone, not having to share. But where was she? Chan chided herself for coming out too early. The auntie would probably still be in bed.

Then she couldn't believe her eyes. Wasn't that her, just emerging from that alley? Chan stood up from the stone wall she was resting on. "Auntie!" she shouted.

The woman spun. Saw her then hurried over. "Chan, child," She was breathing hard. "I was coming to talk to your mother. I have a wonderful idea!"

"What is it, Auntie? Tell me. I was looking for you."

"I should tell your Ma first."

"Tell me," Chan coaxed, seeing that Auntie was pink cheeked with news.

It burst out of her. "You have Papa and I have money." She stood back, eyes sparkling, arms crossed.

"I don't understand," Chan murmured.

Auntie stamped her foot. "They charge a fee to get into the camp and I have the money. I want to go with you. As a relative! Pretend I'm your Papa's sister."

Chan's heart lifted—then as suddenly sank. "But you don't know how to contact the woman, do you? That's why I was looking for you. I wanted to talk to her and maybe..." Her voice lost its strength and words were lost in the rumble of a passing cart.

Auntie, frowned, stared at Chan, then her brows lifted. "No, Child. I know the way. We can all go!"

We can all go—that is all Chanbopha heard and she grabbed Auntie's hand and began to pull her, puffing and wheezing, back to where Ma had just climbed from her bed and was wondering where her daughter was. Chan spilled it all out before Auntie could gather breath enough to speak and Ma excitedly agreed.

Auntie rushed off to arrange matters with the guide who must take them there, while Chan and Ma told the boys.

They waited and waited. Ate their breakfast. Packed everything they owned, then waited some more. The boys stayed home, Chan didn't go to the market and Ma couldn't work on her shawls. What if Auntie got into an accident or couldn't find the address? Chan thought she would burst if she must wait any longer.

Finally Auntie returned. "Tonight," she said. "The guide will meet us here after dark to lead us across the border. It is dangerous. Pol Pot soldiers are always hunting Cambodians trying to escape." She paused as though expecting them to declare it not worth the risk. No one said a word. "Then I must go home and prepare."

That day seemed forever and when at last night came and the neighborhood was quiet they sat hushed until a knock announced the arrival of Thuy and a wiry dark skinned man who seemed nameless. Soon they were six shadows leaving the town.

At first Chan was full of energy but soon, long past bedtime, she grew unbearably sleepy. Sometimes she closed her eyes and walked half asleep. Once she thought she heard someone saying, "We are now in Thailand," and later she wished she'd been awake to remember her last steps in Cambodia.

The thought made her sad and she stopped and looked back along the night road. Ma bent down and whispered one word in her daughter's ear, "Papa".

Chan smiled and quickened her step, looking only forward. Dawn broke and a first bird squawked in the brush. Chan bumped into Vuthy who had stopped at a high, barbed wire and timber gate.

Their guide was met by guards who let him inside, telling the others to wait. The little family, except for Chan, sat wearily where they stood but she leaned against the wire looking into a village.

At first it resembled their old prison camp but as people emerged into early sunlight it became excitingly different. While women swept their doorways children ran out to laugh and play, young girls talked and huddled together, giggling. Girls like her! I will be able to have friends here, thought Chan, and make noise! Maybe go to school! I will learn English so I am ready for America.

Their guide returned. "I gave them money. Someone will come and show you where to go." He left without another word and loped back the way they had come leaving them adrift and nervously wondering what would happen next.

For a long time they stood by the guard house, ignored. It was already hot and flies buzzed. Chan's tummy rumbled. She couldn't remember when she last ate. She had been too excited to think of it.

Michael Odom (Papa)

refugee camp at Khoo-I-Dang

with papers for America

Staff photo by KENNETH SILVER

Dany Pol and her children (left) Vuthy, Chanbopha and Sovirak face difficulties in resettling.

Future uncertain for refugee family

arriving in America

Papa's funeral

wedding day

CHAPTER TWENTY

A commotion startled Chan from half sleep. Four soldiers were glaring at them speaking a dialect she barely understood but from their actions she knew they demanded money. Vuthy and Sovirak insisted the guide had already paid; given everything they had. Chanbopha cringed from the too close muzzle of a rifle. The soldiers insisted; shouting, and then they grabbed Vuthy, stripping the clothes from his body. Searching him. She looked toward the guardhouse for help but those two guards were studiously ignoring what went on behind them. She looked away from the search now of Sovirak and as the boys struggled to re-clothe themselves the guards roughly disrobed Ma and Auntie Thuy, getting ever angrier at finding nothing of value. Rough hands next seized Chan. "Not the child," screamed Ma but the hands bruised and hurt while Chan sobbed more from humiliation than pain.

"Go, march!" The five were shoved forward, rifles herding them into thick woods.

"They are going to kill us." whispered Vuthy. "I understand them. They say there is barely enough food for the refugees who are here—they only take people with much money now."

"But we paid," said Ma, "and they are not Khmer Rouge. I thought we were safe here."

"They are Thai thieves," these last words were forced out by the butt of a rifle between Vuthy's shoulder blades.

They stumbled on. This was a nightmare, it must be, they had reached safety hadn't they? A root tripped Chan and she almost fell into the sunlit glade.

Rifle barrels waved them into line and Ma slipped one hand over Chan's eyes.

Chan held her breath. She had seen so many people killed and dead. Now she would be one of them. She never would see Papa! At that thought her eyes popped open and through cracks between Ma's fingers she saw the soldiers in a line facing them, rifles raised—but she also saw something move behind them.

"Lower your weapons," a voice commanded as five more soldiers emerged from between slender tree trunks.

The leader of the firing squad seemed to be explaining things to this higher ranking officer and Chan recognized the subordinate as the kind of man who liked to kill and she knew that he was disappointed to have been thwarted. She also knew he would never forgive them for eluding him.

She pried Ma's hand from her face. They had all been too surprised to move and now they watched the Captain approach, a tall, handsome man, like Papa, or so Chan thought, immediately liking him. Without thinking she stepped forward and took his hand.

He looked down at her with a slight smile then Ma hissed and yanked her back beside her.

The officer introduced himself as Captain Zaphorn then spoke to them in good Khmer. "I am sorry, it is hard to get good men. They are wild and greedy. They saw your skin is white so think you must be rich." He turned to Ma. "You are very lucky it was time to change the guard or we could not have saved you. These are your children? Where is your husband?"

Ma nodded. "My husband is in the United States. He is an army officer like you and the authorities sent him to a special officer's school. He will send money for us to join him there."

"And his name?"

"Oum. Captain Oum. Michael Oum."

The tall officer clapped his hands together. "I know him. We went to Phnom Penh University together." Smiling like Chanbopha had never thought possible for an officer other than Papa, he grasped her under her armpits and hoisted her up to eye level. She felt warm and happy and wondered why Mama was still cold and shaking.

"Come, we must get you into camp. Why do you hesitate?" he said, for Ma would not move.

"Those soldiers. They will kill us when they see us. They will be angry that you stopped them."

"No, Mrs. Oum, I will see that you have a house next to mine. I will keep you safe until you can go to your husband."

"It's all right Ma," urged Sovirak.

And so they went into the village they had only glimpsed and Chan, was excited to enter the hustle and bustle of a normal day with smells of food cooking and sounds of laughter, a mother scolding her child. The officer took them to a small house next to his bigger one and Chanbopha and the two boys explored it while Ma and Auntie stayed talking to the kind man who had saved their lives. Chan tried not to think about the sight through Ma's fingers of those soldiers leveling their rifles at her but she knew that at every turn in that 'village' she would fear meeting them.

The Captain gave Ma money. "Your husband will repay me in the future. Good day, Mrs. Oum." He glanced around at them all, saluted, smiled at Chan and left.

Pride bubbled in Chanbopha's chest. Even from America Papa's reputation protected them.

"Come Chan, stop dreaming. I know you're tired but first we must buy food. The captain said there is a market nearby. Boys, you go find water so we can wash, have tea and sleep. Tomorrow we will all look for the English school."

Auntie stayed behind to make up the cots with the two sheets and a blanket piled on the end of each. Sovirak and Vuthy went one way, Ma and Chanbopha the other.

Chan skipped and chattered, excited to be among people who looked well fed. The only children she saw were very young but, of course, the older ones were in school, where she'd be tomorrow, learning English. She gave a happy hop but then shrank back as two men in uniform passed. Fear from that dawn chilled her but the soldiers paid them no attention and soon were lost among the crowd. Weariness caught up as Chan accepted the armload of rice, noodles, fresh cabbage and dried fish Ma bought at a small market. Lastly, with a smile, Ma handed her a chocolate bar which looked, from the drawing outside, to be stuffed with shredded coconut. "For you now." she said. "Don't tell the others."

Chan set their purchases on a nearby upturned box and unwrapped her treat. Never had anything tasted so delicious. The chocolate was runny and a maggot waved its head from where Chan had bitten but she barely noticed—she had eaten far worse than that. She nibbled, savoring each bite and chewing each sweet strand of coconut until it dissolved. When her tongue caressed the last lick of chocolate from her upper lip she looked at the wrapper, 'Made in America'. She looked up at Ma who had been watching her with a smile.

A pang of conscience struck. "Oh, Ma, I ate it all! I should have given you half."

"No, Chan, I wanted you to taste America. Some day you will have all the sweets you want. Now pick up our purchases and let's get home."

The next day the two boys and Chanbopha started school. No one studied harder than Chan for she, although almost a teenager, had never been in a serious class with a professional teacher. Just sitting in this orderly row of desks was a joy even though the frozen faced man was so quick to punish with the cane he seldom put down. A vicious slash across her knuckles was nothing to what Chan had previously endured and the thrill of learning seemed well worth it.

Apart from school and necessary trips to buy food or go to the post office the Oum family stayed close to home and

Captain Zaphorn's house for fear the bad soldiers might come looking for them. Ma often visited the Captain's pregnant young wife and Chan wondered if she was reminded of her own dead baby. Especially as, when she came home, she spent a long time at the shrine she had set up in a corner of the room.

Chan was kept busy cleaning the house and studying but the boys were plainly bored and it was just lucky they had school to occupy some of their time.

Weeks passed. Every day Chan ran to the post office positive there would be a letter from Papa, but each day she was disappointed. Ma didn't even need to ask after hearing her daughter's slow steps come in the door. The Captain "loaned" them enough money to buy food and when he came to visit Chan would always ask if Papa had found them yet. Captain Zaphorn would shake his head and explain that with no embassy in this place it was difficult to track people. This camp which had once seemed so hopeful was starting to feel like another prison and even the English teacher, Chan suspected, was not so fluent in English himself when, after covering the basic levels, he began the same course over again.

CHAPTER TWENTY-ONE

Chan arrived home after another fruitless detour to the post office after class. Just inside the door she stopped. Everything they owned lay piled in the middle of the floor and Vuthy and Sovirak were stuffing small things inside bigger things handed to them by Auntie Thuy.

Ma looked up from dismantling her shrine. "Chanbopha, thanks to Buddha you have come! Captain Zaphorn has found another friend of your father who will take us to that better refugee camp called Khoo-I-Dang, further across the Thai border. It is run by the Thai Ministry of the Interior and the United Nations. We will be safer and live with the man's nephews. The oldest boy works at the American embassy, right in the camp."

"We can go straight from there to America!" Vuthy exclaimed. "Go get ready. Pa's friend is coming soon."

It all seemed too good to be true and soon Chan had her own few possessions ready to go. Her heart pounded with excitement. No longer must they fear meeting those soldiers who had almost murdered them. If it hadn't been for Captain Zaphorn they would all be dead and now Ma was next door saying goodbye to his wife. Soon the Captain would see them safely through the gate on their way to be even closer to Papa and America. "Vuthy! Sovirak" she shouted, "Where are you? The uncle will be here any minute."

The boys appeared and dumped their bundles by the door. "Calm down, little sister. Who knows whether the new place will be any better than this."

"But Papa can get us out from there."

"Maybe he won't want to. It's been a long time. He may have another family by now." Sovirak smirked.

Chan stopped breathing then a red cloud blocked her vision and she flew at her brother pummeling him with her fists and kicking his shins. "Papa would never do that," she gasped.

A large pickup's arrival interrupted, drawing them all outside to meet another of Papa's friends, a small wiry man with kind eyes, who bustled them toward the cab of his truck,

Chan began to panic, "Ma! Ma! Wait for Ma!"

But there she came trotting alongside the Captain. He helped her up onto the front seat between the driver and Sovirak who held Chan on his lap and Vuthy jammed against the door, one elbow hanging out the window.

"Auntie. Where's Auntie?" Chan spun her head looking for the woman who had been with them since they'd met in that last town.

"It's okay," said Ma, looking straight ahead. "She has friends here. She will come later."

Chanbopha had a moment of doubt as they sailed through the gate with the Captain's good wishes following them. Then she looked ahead. We're coming, Papa! She heard the engine's throb repeat that phrase over and over.

The country changed to sparsely wooded plains

The road was bumpy and heat glued the five passengers together. They stopped several times to stretch, go behind bushes, drink from a stream or eat fists full of the sticky rice Ma had brought.

Each time Chan hated getting back into the exhaust smelling squish of the pickup and now carsickness was making her woozy. What if she had to vomit and was unable to reach a window!

They stopped again but this time no one got out. Papa's friend had something to say.

"We are almost there. Listen carefully. You will be in this camp illegally until you get the ID tag everyone must wear.

Therefore you will stay hidden. My nephew and his two younger brothers are expecting you. Liu is a good boy so do as he says, and when you get your identification and legal status life will be easier."

Chan's heart sank. She had thought all the bad stuff was over. Imagined that after a short time of being in the new better camp life would begin again in another land and she could be a normal girl.

"It is four-thirty, time when the guards break and only a few work the entrance." He restarted the engine and scraped the vehicle into gear. "My nephew is a smart boy. He has bribed this one to let us in."

Chan strained forward, then quailed when she saw closed gates ahead. Similar ones not so long ago had had thieves and murderers lurking behind them. She held her breath as they swung open, but no guards appeared. Even so, as they drove through Chan squeezed her eyes tight shut so as to be invisible.

They entered what seemed to be a small city built on the lower slope of a high rocky bluff. Between several wide roads radiating from the center, identical thatched bamboo shacks filled every spot of land. There seemed no space between them with only a very few scraggly trees here and there. People swarmed everywhere and Chanbopha leaned across her brothers to see better. She first noticed that each man, woman and child wore a name and address plainly visible on his or her chest. Chan shivered. She did not want to wear one of those. And yet without one, Papa's friend said, they could not stay here. And without living here there could be no America.

They stopped in front of a house where a young man waited. Quickly he stepped forward, greeted his uncle and tugged open the truck's door, introducing himself as Liu Chea before hustling them out, up some steps and into a large room. Only then did he smile. "Sorry, but we need to keep your presence secret for a while." He ordered two boys, younger versions of himself, to bring in the Oums' belongings.

The sound of an engine rattling into action outside caused Chan to leap toward the door but Liu's firm hand on her arm stopped her.

"But the Uncle's leaving. We must thank him. Say goodbye!" Chan pleaded. Strange how she felt no emotion when treated cruelly but now any act of kindness brought her to the verge of tears.

The brown eyes of the young man smiled although his face was stern. "You can thank him when he comes back in a week or so. Don't worry, Chanbopha, he understands."

Chan relaxed. She could trust this boy/man. Already she felt the load of responsibility shifting from her shoulders.

She turned to look at the one big room. Where were the seven of them going to sleep, she saw no beds.

Liu called for attention. "Please listen, what I have to say is very important. As you see everyone in the camp is wearing their name and address always in plain view." He pointed to his own and those on the chests of his two brothers. "This is so that bad people can not come in and cause trouble. Until I get yours for you we must keep your presence secret. If you are discovered you will be sent back to Cambodia and I will be severely punished."

Chan drew in a sharp breath. In her experience severe punishment meant torture or death.

Liu continued. "I have prepared a place under the floor where you can hide during the day when officials often make surprise visits. As I work at the embassy I have ways to get you registered so after a few weeks you will be free to lead a normal life." He then pointed to one side of the room. "Over there are two hammocks for my brothers and a bed for me. On the other side are hammocks for Sovirak and Vuthy and a big bed for Auntie Oum and Chanbopha to share. During the day the hammocks are hung out of the way while the two beds can be used to sit on."

Chanbopha couldn't help smiling to herself at how proud he was of his planning of this space which must have been only just enough for him and his brothers before the arrival of four others.

"The communal latrine is halfway down the street," he continued, "And every day a truck brings water from which we fill our buckets and containers. The school here is very good too. Now you must eat." He pointed to a table dividing the two sleeping areas. Seven crates served as chairs

Liu had prepared a good meal in the tiny kitchen Chan saw at the back of the big room. Through its small window she could see the rear wall of another house, almost touching theirs. She guessed it must face another street. At first, after feeling so carsick, she feared she couldn't manage even a mouthful of the fish Liu said he'd caught that morning but after a few tentative bites she felt better and would have had more but for the startling interruption of a loudspeaker.

"Section nine! Section nine!"

"That's us," said Liu, putting down his chopsticks and cocking his head to listen.

"Report of violent nighttime robberies make it imperative you leave your homes immediately. Hide all valuables and proceed to the hospital where you will be safe. Do this every night until the danger is over. Evacuate now!" The message was spoken in Khmer but with an American accent. Chan reminded herself that this camp was run by foreigners which, because the refugees were all Cambodian, was easy to forget.

Chan looked to Liu for direction.

"Carry your burdens high to hide your chest so no one can see you have no number," Liu whispered.

Calm and authoritative, he was someone to trust. and they all did as he said, snatching up their still bundled possessions. Surrounded by their new protector and his brothers, they went outside.

It was to Chanbopha as though she was thrust into reliving a long ago nightmare. Frightened people shoved and jostled, trampled her feet and pushed with bruising elbows as they fled along a dark street. A scream rose in Chan's throat but a small voice in her head stifled it; soothed and reasoned. There are no bodies here with their heads bashed in, no dead babies in the ditch, no Khmer Rouge shooting and beating. No, Chan, this is not like then. The voice calmed her and she took a deep breath, releasing the tight grip she'd had on Ma's hand.

Liu looked down at her and smiled. "Brave girl," he said as though he read her thoughts.

Liu's two words revived her faith in herself. She would get Ma and the boys beyond all this. She may be small and a child but she was tough and smart. For just a moment she had forgotten.

They reached a big building which was the hospital and there they were told to find a spot on the lawn on which to spend the night. Ma found a couple of shawls for herself and Chan and the boys used jackets for pillows. A wave of weariness overcame Chanbopha. She barely had energy to swat away the hungry mosquitoes until she vaguely felt herself being covered with some cloth to thwart them. "It'll be all right," she whispered sleepily to Ma lying next to her... and she didn't even snatch the tail of a dream that night.

CHAPTER TWENTY-TWO

They were sent home very early in the morning, hustling through streets in a reversal of the night before. Liu met them at the door, the boys having beaten Ma and Chan with an earlier start. They ate breakfast then Chan was puzzled when Liu herded them toward an opening in the floor. "No," she said, planting her feet. "We will not go down there."

"You must," Liu said, severe lines bracketing his mouth.

"No! Ma?" Why weren't the others backing her up?

"We must do as Liu says. He understands this place." Ma's voice was calm. "We are not legal here."

"Your Mother is right. Remember, if you are caught you will be sent back to Cambodia. Also I will be punished. Please?"

Chan looked into Liu's brown eyes and instead of the man saw a boy not many years older than Vuthy, beseeching her to obey. Sadness fell over her like a fog. These past terrible years of the Pol Pot had murdered Liu's childhood as it had hers but they had lived while the regime killed off so many. Somewhere there must still be a life worth living. How could she betray this kind young man and her family now just because the thought of being shut underground terrified her? With a sigh and a shrug she walked to the hole and climbed down the waiting ladder. Ma, Sovirak and Vuthy followed.

Liu leaned down handing Ma a lantern but it was Chanbopha he spoke to. "There is food and water in the box and a bucket in the corner. After the guards have come through, which could be late afternoon, I will release you. They only come once each day. Two weeks and I will have numbers for you. I am sorry!"

And Chan knew he really was sorry as he backed away and lowered the floor. The four hunkered close together on splintery wooden crates and listened in silence to something being dragged over the trap door to hide its presence. No one moved. Chan fought the creeping edges of claustrophobia then in her head she heard Liu's voice, "Brave girl," he had said yesterday. She remembered the pride those words had lit in her and felt it again. "Well," she said, to the others. "What game shall we play?"

That was the longest day ever. They sat crammed together, taking turns to stretch out their legs. In the dim light of a candle they played games, did math sums, recited poetry and made up stories. Ma taught them how to meditate. Chan fell asleep.

Scraping above their heads alerted them to the arrival of freedom and the opening of the trap door brought them blinking into the light. Liu's two young brothers looked on as Chan was first out, handed up to Liu by Vuthy. She smelled food and saw that Liu had prepared what seemed a feast, but first they all had to wash and use the outhouse. Liu watched anxiously as they ate and Chan stuffed herself to show appreciation.

Soon they were scurrying through the streets again for another night at the hospital. This time it was harder for Chan to sleep as she had already slept many hours during the day, so she looked up at the stars and imagined Papa looking at the same ones and getting his home ready for his family's arrival.

And so it continued for six days and nights. As time passed they became resigned to the safety of their hiding place and used to sleeping on hospital grass.

On the seventh evening, as they were preparing to head out for the night, they were surprised to hear the preliminary attention-getting tweets of the loudspeaker. Then it boomed, freezing everyone in place. "Section nine. Stay in your huts. Emergency over. Section nine stay in your huts."

"Did they catch the robbers then?" whispered Chanbopha.

Everyone looked toward Liu. "Who knows. But we must all be careful. Trust no one. There are many kinds of people in here, good and bad. Some very bad."

But you will protect us, thought Chan. and all the trust she had once put into her adopted older brother Vuthy she transferred to this serious young man who had taken charge of their lives.

For the first time in this camp, the Oum family slept under a roof and in beds, or hammocks as it was for the boys. Chan awoke often to listen for footsteps but all she heard were the soft snores of sleepers interspersed by whimpers probably caused by someone's nightmarish repeats of Khmer Rouge horrors.

On the morning of the ninth day as they sat down for their hasty breakfast before hiding, Chanbopha noticed a piece of cardboard at her place.

She saw the same in front of Ma, Vuthy and Sovirak. Quickly she turned hers over." Chanbopha Oum -Section 9-101". She looked up, questioning. Liu was watching with a small smile on his usually serious face. "You are now legal residents," he said.

Ma and her brothers were looking at theirs.

"We're free?" whispered Chan.

Liu nodded. "To go anywhere in the camp."

"No more cave?"

"No more."

Chan now fingered the ID tag she had dreaded having to wear. Now it was a magic key. Her siblings and Ma were smiling. Chan's began and grew until it made her cheeks ache and she started jumping up and down with excitement.

"Hold still." Liu was trying to pin her tag to her t-shirt. "Now you legally belong here. But wear it always. Promise?" His brown eyes willed her to obey.

After a moment she nodded. Then she whirled and ran out through the door and into the street.

Freedom! How wonderful to be out in the sunshine amongst people who sometimes smiled and greeted each other. There was very little motorized traffic on the paved road where bicycles and scooters travelled carefully among pedestrians. The air smelled of hot dust and wood smoke—and always in the background music played over a loud-speaker. She hadn't noticed it at first but there it was, a continuous beat. Chan wandered, happily exploring, until her stomach reminded her of the breakfast she had been about to eat.

Every house being a replica of its neighbors she couldn't recognize hers and turned in confused circles,

"Chanbopha! Chanbopha!"

The high shrill calls cut through to her and she saw Liu's two young brothers on the porch she had just passed. She sucked in a deep breath of relief, and jumped the steps two at a time to pass them and go inside.

"You got yourself lost, didn't you! Lucky we saw you!" The youngest accused behind her. "Your Ma and Liu are really mad at you running off like that."

"Was not lost," she said. They had never liked having to share their living space and big brother with another family, she knew that, but it wasn't her fault.

The days developed a routine. Up at five when the boys fetched buckets of water from the truck at the top of their section and Chan cleaned and tidied the house. Everyone washed while Ma made breakfast. Chan hadn't realized that Liu went to work at the Embassy at the other end of camp every day from nine to five. "How do you think I got your cards?" he reminded when she asked where he was going in a clean shirt and trousers. The embassy also gave out rice, vegetables and chicken to the refugees and Liu brought their ration home with him in the evening. When Chan learned this she realized that he had been sharing his with them before they became recognized members of the camp. No wonder the younger boys had resented their presence.

Fuller stomachs made them much friendlier and they escorted Chan and her brothers to school, proud to show them the ropes. Chan was excited to find that this was real school;

teaching math, science and history. Not what she would have been learning in Cambodia but the boys said she would get a high school certificate if she passed the final tests and that high marks might make it easier to attain acceptance to America. Chanbopha immediately set that goal for herself and hoped Vuthy and Sovirak were doing the same.

CHAPTER TWENTY-THREE

The roomful of students turned and stared when they entered. Chan's mouth was so dry she could barely tell the teacher her name. Many of the children were older and may have been coming for a while but Chan was determined to catch up and from that first day she studied every spare moment and, thanks to Ma's patient coaching, she would soon find herself on a level with the best. Few of these children had such a diligent parent but also, many came from much humbler families whose parents had never attended school themselves. Most of the more highly educated people had been exterminated by the Pol Pot and sometimes Chan wondered if perhaps the fact that Papa had not been with his family was all that saved them from the same fate.

That first noon, when they ran home for lunch, Chan was bubbling with news, and eager to go back to an afternoon of English. Ma came with them to this class and Chan could see by her smile that she was happier than she'd been in a long while. The only flaw was that Liu's youngest brother refused to accompany them. "I don't want to learn English." He sat stubbornly on the porch step and would say nothing more. It reminded Chan of Srey refusing to eat and was the only cloud on that day.

It took a month for him to be persuaded but finally the six of them went to English lessons every weekday afternoon and each evening Chan taught Liu what she had learned.

On Saturdays they shopped at the market spending some of the money brought by Liu's uncle on the first Sunday of each month. He said it was a loan until Papa heard where they were and they showed their gratitude by cooking him the best breakfast they could produce. They'd hear the old truck arriving early in the morning and run to meet it, then Liu's always cheerful uncle would sit down with them and eat while telling news from the outside world. Amazing things like artificial hearts and a shuttle called Challenger which carried men into space where one walked in the middle of the sky! Chan was excited to hear that a movie actor named Ronald Reagan was president of the United States and she wondered if Papa knew him.

But what joy on the day Uncle told them the money this time was from Papa! It had arrived already changed from U.S. currency to Thai Baht through something called federal express. "Papa has found us!" was all Chan could think. "He has found us!"

After that on the days Uncle arrived Chan barely heard anything he said as she waited for the moment when he reached into his pocket. "And your father sent this," he'd say as coins clattered onto the table.

For many visits Chan was hesitant about voicing her biggest hope, then one Sunday she whispered, "No letter?"

Everyone went quiet

Uncle's hands stopped moving and after a long pause he said, "Your Father's a busy man with his life in America. You must be grateful he finds time to send the money, Child."

Ma broke in, "And we are grateful to you, Uncle, for providing a safe place for him to send it. For sure it would be stolen at the camp post office."

And so they talked about other things while Chanbopha listened to none of it but seethed with anger against the father she had loved and fought to reach through all those terrible times. Now he had found them he was too busy to even send a note.

That morning she didn't go out to watch the old truck rattle away. She used to imagine how someday she would be on it going out that gate on her way to a real life. Now hope had drained away and left her empty. Papa didn't care.

But life went on in spite of the new sad spot in Chan's heart. They knew people to say hello to when she and Ma shopped and they chatted with their neighbors. Most were poorer than they and scrambled for ways to get by. One family made tofu and when Chan was sent to buy some she often played a game of pick-up sticks with the family's two teenage sons. As soon as they saw her coming they would gather as many chopsticks as they could find, and pick a plump lime from the struggling little tree nearby, Then they beckoned her to join them. Chan enjoyed sitting on the floor cross legged, taking her turn to throw the lime high and, while it was in the air, snatching up one stick without disturbing any others before catching the lime on its way down. Chan usually won by collecting the most sticks but refused the prize citrus, knowing that she was wealthy compared to these people. She had noticed that the boys had only one shirt each whereas she and her brothers each had three.

Across the way were a husband and wife who sold bananas. They argued loudly and their fights caused much laughter in the neighborhood. Chan suspected their altercations were put on like a show to amuse the watchers and gain attention. She had seen people give a tad extra for the bananas they bought from them.

All the section nine people, knew each other. Periodically someone would disappear and whispers would spread. "American uncle, Australian cousins."

Hearing this Chanbopha would think, "American father" and something would ache deep inside her as she reminded herself she could no longer count on him.

Liu's uncle brought him a bicycle which made getting to and from work at the embassy faster. Often in the evenings Chan was allowed to ride it up and down the nearby streets and sometimes Liu would ask her to help him mend a broken chain or flat tire. His praise when they finished lifted her for a short time from her recent feelings of uselessness and lack of purpose.

Other teenage girls were allowed to wander freely with their friends and Chan often fought with her mother. "Why can't I go with them? You let Vuthy and Sovirak do whatever they want. Sometimes I hear them come in near dawn and they smell of beer."

Ma would frown. "They are men now. You are my daughter and because I love you I keep you safe. Trust me."

So Chan stayed home, studied and cleaned and listened to the talk when neighbors came over to play cards with Ma. They reported on who had caught the ever lurking fever spread by mosquitoes and who survived. Often Chan didn't fully understand what they said but it seemed much went on in camp to be gossiped about. A girl had just died mysteriously and this was discussed in whispers as though it was shameful and not for Chan to know about. She pretended to be reading and deduced it must be some terrible disease there was no medicine for. She wondered how contagious it was. Perhaps she had stood next to that same girl in school!

When she awoke next morning with a terrible ache in her stomach she was sure she had caught "it". She struggled through her chores, tired and aching, puzzled whether to tell Ma she was dying. Ma had seemed so happy lately Chan couldn't bear to cause her more sorrow. Also if she complained she would be made to stay home and today was the exam she had studied so hard for. Whatever happened she was going to do that test! Good marks would make Ma smile even if her daughter did die.

"What is the matter? You are so pale, Chanbopha and your eyes so small?"

"I am fine thank you, Teacher," Chan tried to read the test paper slid in front of her. It kept blurring in and out of focus but she knew the answers and concentrated against the waves of pain and sleepiness: whatever happened she must finish. The terrible fever that girl died of was consuming her. She was sweating, all over, so even the chair beneath her was wet. She slid a hand under her and it came away red. "Oh, my, I am bleeding to death," She panicked, only two questions to go.

She raised her hand.

"Are you finished, Chanbopha? Bring it here then."

"Please, Teacher, I feel very bad. Can I go home please?" She could not possibly go up there in front of the whole class, her shorts covered in blood.

The teacher came to her, thank goodness, took the papers and told Chan she could leave. Chanbopha slung her back pack low to cover the incriminating evidence of her fatal disease and ran home as fast as she could to burst in on her surprised Ma with the news that she was dying.

"Oh my little Chan!"

Why was Ma smiling?

"I forgot to tell you—you still seem so young but of course you are thirteen. This happens to all girls when we change into women..."

All of a sudden Chan didn't feel so sick. She didn't like it but it was okay. Ma got out an old sarong and cut strips from it which Chan must wear and wash to always have a clean one ready.

That night in bed Chan thought about her day and how glad she was not to be dying. Instead of making Ma cry she had made her laugh! For a moment she was grateful she had not been older for this to happen in the prison camp where Ma had no extra sarong to cut up. She rolled over. The cramps had gone.

CHAPTER TWENTY-FOUR

Twice a year for three days the whole camp celebrated the Khmer New Year; first on April thirteenth, fourteenth and fifteenth, next on Sept. fifteenth, sixteenth and seventeenth. These traditional festive days started with a great flurry of house cleaning after which Chan accompanied Ma to market. There they would buy the foods designated by Buddha's Angel as reported over the camp's loudspeaker. Back home they set out the mangoes, oranges, bananas, lychee and longan, two plates of each—always two—no more no less. There were also special candies from Thailand and two vases of flowers.

That first year when Chan stood looking at the colorfully laden table the boys had placed on the porch outside their front window, she felt a surge of joy as though she were seeing anew something she had once loved but never expected to experience again. Everyone was happy to be following the old ways as though the years of communism had never been, but it also caused sadness by awakening memories of those who had died. How very many!. Neighbors dropped in and the adults gossiped over cards while children played outside and everyone ate what Ma had cooked that morning.

At night Liu offered to help Chan clean up so Ma could go to bed after her long day. He made her laugh so much as they worked that Chan was sorry when there was nothing left to do. For a while she even forgot that she wanted to leave this camp and stop being a refugee. As she tidied away a few last things, she heard the rustle of Liu's bed in the far corner of the room and smiled. He was such a kind man and surely handsomer than President Reagan. Tonight he had seemed quite young, almost a boy in fact. Chanbopha drifted off to sleep wondering if somewhere Papa had also been celebrating. But she tried not to think of him anymore,

On Day two they all went to temple and Chan prayed for change. She prayed so hard her finger nails dug into her palms and although she knew Buddha taught patience she believed she had shown him enough of that. Please, let it be our turn to leave this Khoo-I-Dang, she pleaded, thinking of all the empty seats in the class room left by others who had been given their papers and gone to a new life.

Day three was family day when everyone stayed home and rested. No school, and no work at the embassy for Liu. Chan gave Ma the new sarong she had saved up for from the small allowance given her each month. It was wonderful to see her mother's eyes light up when she saw it but why didn't anyone speak of leaving anymore? Whenever she asked Liu about it he said it was up to their father to petition for their release. But Papa didn't care. Was she the only one to understand that? He sent money every month but who was to prove he even did that? Liu's uncle was a kind man...

Their fifth Khmer New year, which was their third year in Khoo-I-Dang. was celebrated with the usual enthusiasm. At first Chan held back thinking herself too grown up for the children's games. After all she must be fifteen now, although as birthdays were not celebrated in Cambodian culture no one was ever quite sure how old they were. But even if the adults did ask her to join them playing cards, sitting with them seemed an unspeakably dull alternative.

"Come on!" Liu circled his arm around her waist and thrust her into the pack of screaming, laughing youngsters.

No hesitancy now, Chan raced and tussled with the wildest of them. At one point in the catch 'em game Liu caught her and, holding her wrists firmly behind her back with one hand, with the other drew on her face with one of Ma's lipsticks.

Everyone watched and giggled and pointed until at last she was let go and proceeded to scrub her face with her bare hands. Everyone ran off after the next victim and in a moment she ran with them.

"You know what Liu wrote on your face?" giggled a girl from school later when they paused to eat cake and drink the sweet lemonade.

"No, he made a mess, that's all I know."

"He wrote, I love you. 'I' on the right cheek, 'love' across your forehead and 'you' on the left cheek."

"He's always joking." Chan, hot with embarrassment, wandered over to stand next to Ma and a cousin visiting from a neighboring section. As soon as she could she left them to scrub her face with soap and water but before all trace was gone she looked in a mirror and tried to find the words Liu had written. They were all gone into one big smudge but peering closely she thought she could almost see them. Chan sighed and finished the job.

Ma called for her to make more tea and she ran into the kitchen and poured water into the kettle. Liu was there putting more sticks on the fire but Chan pretended not to notice, hoping her cheeks weren't crimson, and when she spoke to him later she avoided his eyes. She told herself she was silly to be so glad he had not written on anyone else's face, but she was. She just wished she'd been able to read it better for herself.

CHAPTER TWENTY-FIVE

Each weekend almost everyone went to the market which was held in the open space from which all the sections radiated. Everyone who had anything to sell brought fruits and vegetables grown on tiny plots or harvested from some nearby tree, clothes children had grown out of, or once treasured mementos sacrificed for more necessary provisions. There were also goods smuggled in from Thailand, which seemed another world to Chanbopha for, although the refugee camp was actually in Thailand, it might as well, due to its Khmer inhabitants, have been a piece of Cambodia.

Chan loved to go and look at all the things she could not afford. This time Ma accompanied her and they stopped in front of a stall displaying a colorful array of materials. A sour looking woman sat half hidden in the corner.

"How beautiful!" said Chan. "Smell, Ma, they are new."

The woman got up and came toward them. "Mrs. Oum," she said. "Are these not fine fabrics—straight from Thailand they are."

"Cousin! I did not know you were here. And how is your husband?"

Ma seemed happy to see this woman but Chan had learned not to be influenced by Ma's joyous reactions on first seeing someone after a long separation. It took a while to recall if she had even liked that person long ago.

"He is well." The woman waved her hands over the goods in front of her. "Always the smart businessman." For a moment she glanced gloomily at the laden tables, then she looked up and rearranged her face. "And this must be little Chanbopha, who I saw as a baby."

Chan smiled at this relative she had no memory of and followed Ma on down the aisle. Looking back she saw the woman retiring back to her hidden chair.

Five days later a large, dark skinned man appeared at their door and introduced himself as the material seller's husband.

Ma invited him in.

"I have come with a job offer for my pretty cousin here." His thick lips smiled at Chan. "You saw my stand at the market. Beautiful materials but nothing sold. Not one piece." His bushy eyebrows pinched into an angry line and Chan imagined him roaring his displeasure. "My wife has no stomach for selling but you are lively and pretty. I think you are a good salesperson. I will pay you well. You would like some money, eh?"

Chan eagerly accepted, imagining herself in a dress made from that same material. Perhaps too, she would buy a new pen and some colored pencils with her earnings. And her first lipstick. What a thrill to have real money! Ma readily agreed.

Next weekend Chan was at the booth early, telling passersby about her fine fabric and how beautiful the women would look in sarongs made of such excellent cloth. She enjoyed standing in the aisle, talking and smiling, seeing the piles of material shrink until the table top showed through and the little box in back filled with money.

At the same time Ma and Liu had started a small noodle business where they could work together serving customers on weekends when the embassy was closed. Ma prepared the noodles at home during the week and it was fun comparing sales and experiences on Sunday nights. Chan was happy.

For four weekends she did this, proudly watching as at the end of the day Cousin appeared and counted each satang. She expected he would pay her at the end of one month but when he didn't she thought it might be every five weeks.

On the fifth Sunday after he had finished counting he patted Chan on her shoulder. "Fine job, little Chan. You will be a sharp business woman when you grow up and leave this place. I have given you priceless training, no? You sold all I have so I thank you." He left her standing there.

"But Cousin," she called after him.

He never looked back.

" Ma," she said when she got home. "He promised to pay me but he gave me nothing. Not even a yard of material. I want to find him, make him pay."

"Let it go child." Ma stroked her daughter's cheek. "You don't want to cause trouble and I think he could do that for us in here. Remember he is family. Though distant I admit. Accept this as a lesson. And you did learn how to sell; that was good. Now go wash. Chicken soup is ready for dinner." Chan scrubbed her face with pent up fury while promising herself to never again trust anyone, especially relatives, in business.

The market closed for the monsoon season and Chan was glad not to have to walk past the stalls feeling upset about what had happened and sad about the material, pen and colored pencils she had never been able to buy. Ma and Liu didn't continue their noodle business either.

They never saw "Cousin" or his wife in that camp again but heard rumors that they had gone to the United States. Had Papa sponsored them? They were his kin too. The very suspicion made Chanbopha so angry she sat down immediately and wrote a letter.

CHAPTER TWENTY-SIX

Dear Papa,

This is your daughter Chanbopha. Thank you very much for the money you send each month. We are healthy and well because of it.

But Oh, Papa, when will you send the petition to get us papers for America? This is not a good place to live, so crowded and with nothing to keep people busy. Also bad people have moved in and every day there is violence and crime. No future here. Please rescue us.

Your daughter, Chanbopha

PS I got top marks in the last test in school. My English is good too.

"Please send this to Papa." Chan handed the licked, stamped and addressed envelope to Liu's uncle just before he left on his next visit. For a moment he looked at Chan as if about to say something, then he nodded, and without a word drove away.

Chan watched him go. They had been here over three years. Most of the refugees with relatives outside to sponsor them had left long ago. Newcomers had taken over their huts allowing them to become ramshackle and filthy. Most of these recent arrivals were untrustworthy and loud, letting their children run about half dressed and unsupervised, stealing food wherever they found it.

School graduation was close. Chanbopha was top of her class and would receive her diploma to prove it. All the family would be proud of her and she would step from her classroom—to what... The same streets, same household chores. No more pick up sticks. Those boys and their parents were long gone. English lessons still filled the afternoons but they did not advance. Each day was like a stagnant pond in which she floundered seeing no way out.

The money still came with no word from the father Chan had trusted and then given up on. But the graduation ceremony brought new resolve. The diploma in her hands signified an ending but didn't an ending mean a new beginning? And that could only be in America. She knew that. She could not give up now. Whether Papa wanted them or not he was the only one who could get them there and as Chan left the stage she swore that whatever it took she would make him do it.

Hence a second letter.

Dear Papa,

Why do you not write? I am your daughter. Have you forgotten us? Do you live alone or do you have a new family that wants you to forget us? Please save us.
I wait to hear from you
Chanbopha.

Chanbopha's spirits flew sky high. She had a mission and knew she would succeed.

When a letter did come she could hardly believe it, and just stared at the envelope Liu's uncle held out to her. Then she searched his face, but his eyes were happy, not teasing. Tentatively she reached out and took it; studied her own name. "Thank you," she whispered and ran behind the house to read before her Ma and brothers knew.

Chan read it over and over. Papa's own handwriting! She stroked her forefinger over the two words then held the paper to her nose breathing in Papa's scent.

Dear Chanbopha,

"Getting the four of you papers is more difficult than you imagine but I continue to try. Be patient my daughter.
You ask if I have another family. Of course not.
Be a good girl, Papa.

Chan read it over and over trying to see behind the lines. How could she be anything but a good girl in this place! Years and years of being patient while others had moved on. How long did it take for a man to make a life in America and bring his family to him? If he wanted to. If he wanted to. Why would he not but for another woman who did not want them there. She felt a lie behind his denial.

Dear Papa,
Your letter made me very happy Could you send me photographs of yourself in your new home? I would so enjoy to see what an American house looks like.
Your obedient and loving daughter,
Chan.

She ran out and gave it to Liu's uncle as he was leaving.

She had to wait two months for Papa's answer and this time Liu's uncle handed her a fat little package. She took it to a quiet corner while the others sat at the table drinking tea and listening to news of the outside world. She heard something as she passed about the space shuttle exploding—killing everyone on board—but at the moment what she held in her hands was much more exciting.

The first photo was of a most wonderful house, with no others pressed close! It even had green grass and flowers with no sign of traffic either human or otherwise. Father must have become rich to have such a mansion all to himself.

Other pictures took her inside. Everything was spotless and modern beyond anything Chan had ever seen. The kitchen gleamed with taps that presumably brought water all the way indoors! What luxury! Papa in blue jeans and an open necked striped shirt was in several photos wearing a satisfied smile but seeming somehow diminished without his army uniform.

Chanbopha brushed aside this small disappointment and went back to the first picture. This wonderful American house was going to be her home! There it waited all furnished and ready. But why then were they still here in this tiny cramped hut in this noisy, crowded, smelly camp of people who had lost everything?

Chan studied the photos again, peering closely. And there in the one of the living room her eyes fastened on a framed portrait propped up on a table. She took the image near the window where light fell on it. A family smiled into the camera; a plump blond woman, two young boys and a small girl held in the arms of a man. Papa!

Chanbopha went cold all over. For an instant everything went black. Papa did have another family! He did not want them to join him. Now she knew! But maybe she was wrong—jumping to conclusions. She must consult an adult. Not Ma. Auntie Thuy who had helped them get to the first camp then later followed them here. She would see that Chan was wrong.

People chatting on their porches seemed not to notice her as she ran past, up her street and down the next. Auntie Thuy was home and hardly had time to say hello before Chan thrust the photo in front of her with a jumbled, panicked question.

The surprised woman spent a long time looking closely at that far away living room. Finally she stood back and sighed. "Yes, he has a new family."

"What are you talking about?" Ma had come in unnoticed.

Auntie held out the photo and Chan didn't breathe while Ma looked, leaned closer. Finally she backed away. "You are wrong! I will write and ask him to swear by Buddha to the truth. He is my husband. He would never desert us. You will see. Come Chan."

Chan followed her mother home, miserable because in her heart she knew her suspicions were true, but longing for Ma to be right.

Back at the hut she threw herself across the bed while Ma, without a word, sat down at the table and wrote. Chan lay listening to the scratching of the pen.

She was awakened by her mother roughly shaking her shoulder. "You put this in an envelope and take it to the post office." A paper was waved in front of her half open eyes. "You made a mistake. All will be well. Papa is an honorable man. Didn't Liu's uncle tell us how he is helping Cambodians in this place called Myrtle Beach?" Then, leaving the letter, Ma went out and Chan knew that for all her bravado Ma was scared.

Chan read the note Ma had written.

My husband, tell me as you would swear to heaven that you have no new family. Tell me the truth. I know to have many wives is the custom in Cambodia but one we never followed, and you are in America now.

Your legal and honorable, wife

Chanbopha tucked the letter into an envelope, addressed it in English bold print to be sure of no mistake, and ran as fast as she could to the post office at the far end of the camp.

The building was a little larger but no less shabby than any of the dwellings nearby. She recognized it by the soldier posted at the door and his presence backed her opinion that having Pa's money sent here would have been a mistake. This simple letter going out, however, would not be tampered with. She bought a stamp, stuck it on then asked three people to make sure of the right slot before popping the envelope in.

CHAPTER TWENTY-SEVEN

Even though it was impossible for there to be a reply so soon, Chanbopha went to the post office the very next day. And every day after that. She also haunted the Embassy asking if papers allowing them into America had arrived. Now in both places officials shook their heads as soon as they saw her.

Only Liu noticed how little she ate and brought home special foods and sweets to encourage her. "You must eat, little Chan. You need to be strong to go to the U.S. or they will not let you in."

But Chan, jolted from the limbo of hopelessness she had been in when she stopped believing in Pa, could not stay still. She no longer saw a future filled with emptiness and felt that by expending energy she could force things to happen. Even the "no" from the officials each day and having to disappoint the question in her mother's eyes was all right. "Tomorrow", she would say, "One of these tomorrows, Ma, we will hear something."

Ma lost weight and when Liu's uncle did not show up at the beginning of the month with Pa's money even the boys knew something was wrong and had to be told.

For three months there came no word. The house was quiet and Chan's visits to the post office grew farther apart although she still believed in tomorrow. Ma had put aside bits of money when it had been regularly arriving but the supply had dwindled to a few coins kept for emergencies. For staples they relied on food provided by the authorities. Chan spent time studying her old English lessons and forced out any doubts that shadowed the edge of her consciousness.

There had been a thunder storm during the night and steam rose like smoke around the messenger who arrived on his motorbike to deliver the request for them to appear at the Embassy. Chan read and reread the note. All she could think was that Papa had done it! Everything was forgiven! The silence had been because he was working on getting them through all the bureaucracy not because he'd forgotten them! He'd probably sent a letter which got lost. All these thoughts galloped through Chan's mind as she put on her best shorts and t-shirt "I'm sorry, Pa," she whispered, regretting all her recent bad thoughts.

Together, with Ma in her newest sarong, they set off. Chan felt grown up and important, as though they had suddenly come into a fortune and no longer belonged to this impoverished world of hopelessness. She, Chanbopha, would soon be living in that grand house in Myrtle Beach and bringing to life all her dreams; the dreams which had kept her going through all those terrible years. Vuthy and Sovirak were excited and had wanted to come also but Liu said two were enough as the office for emigration was not very big.

Ma and Chan walked past the guards at the Embassy door and were shown into a small room crowded with two frail chairs and a very large desk. Behind this, in a much larger chair, sat a plump, very white American whose horn rimmed spectacles had lenses which shrank his eyes to the size of lentils.

He did not ask them to sit down so they stood awkwardly behind the two chairs while he shuffled papers. "You have been seeking permission to go to the United States?"

Chan nodded, proud to have understood her first real American. The officials at the front desk were Khmer so when they had spoken American on Chan's previous frequent visits it really sounded more like her own language, but this was different. This was the real thing!

The official separated one paper from the file. "I must inform you that permission has been denied."

The room was silent. Somewhere in the distance a man laughed.

"Denied?" Chan's whisper was scarcely audible. Had she learned that word? Perhaps learned it wrongly?

"Why? That cannot be!" said Ma.

The official closed his eyes. "You have been denied entry as the man you say is your husband has another family. You have a certificate to prove your marriage?"

Ma collapsed in a faint and at the ting of a bell a secretary rushed in and helped Chan place Ma in a chair. Then the woman left for a glass of water.

"How many refugees here have papers?" Chan boiled with rage. "The Khmer Rouge did not allow us to keep papers—we were lucky to keep our lives! You are supposed to help us not imprison us!" This American may not understand her language perfectly but he could not mistake the fury in her Khmer words. Then to her horror she burst into sobs. Every instinct urged her to turn and run, far and forever, into some dark peace away from people.

The official had come from behind his desk and was patting her shoulder. "Stop it, Child. I said your Mother cannot go but you can. You and your brother are your father's children, and when you reach legal age you can sponsor your mother and maybe the other boy who lives with you. Vuthy is it?"

The man was just a blurry figure through Chanbopha's eyes and his words an incomprehensible jumble. Ma shifted in her chair.

The official leaned down, reaching for Chan's shoulder. "You hear me? You and Sovirak can go to America. Next week maybe. I have your visas in my desk"

He smelled bad. His smile looked like a cat's. Chanbopha stepped away from his hand. Now she could clearly see into his lentil eyes. She understood what he said this time and there wasn't enough room in her mouth for all the words wanting to spew out. Finally some came. "Sir, yes, it is my dream to go to my father but I would never leave Ma or Vuthy. We are family and we have come a long and hard way to get here. We have seen terrible things and Ma has watched two children die."

Ma straightened and opened her eyes.

"We have survived on hope and the dream of joining Papa. I would never leave them now—halfway to nowhere. We will go back to Phnom Penh."

With that she took hold of Ma's arm and pulled her to her feet.

The official put out a hand to stop them. "No, no. I will have a car take you home. I think she is unwell beyond shock. I will have a doctor sent to see her." He held the door open and a soldier supported Ma to the car already waiting. Chan refused to get in; the boys would help Ma once she got there, but Chan needed to run—to settle the demons in her head and start planning their return to Cambodia.

CHAPTER TWENTY-EIGHT

To Pa:

You are a Liar! ! Why did you lie? In my heart you died! I began not to trust you when you took so long to get us with you. I asked for house photos to find truth. I asked, but I already knew.

Okay, I don't want to bother you in the US or make problems. Just please send money for us to get back to Cambodia. Ma has heart problems. We cannot walk all that way to Phnom Penh. There is nowhere else to go. Chanbopha

Chan wrote in English just to show Pa she could.

Again she waited but this time it was with dread of the problems they must face after, and if, the money arrived. She sat down with an old map to plan their route but after a short while gave it up in frustration. Perhaps Liu's uncle would know about such things as trains and buses.

Ma slept a lot although the doctor said her heart was all right now if she was careful. Chan thought Ma was just depressed. Vuthy and Sovirak were out a lot with their friends and Liu came and went with a heavy quietness about him. His younger brothers had developed a passion for soccer so spent many hours busy with things connected with their teams and Chan was relieved to have them out of the house. Now the boys were almost men their one room hut was over-crowded and Chan, now fifteen, longed for privacy and a mirror in which she could practice hair styles and try a little lipstick and perhaps eye pencil like other girls she saw. Once a boy had said she was pretty and she wanted to know if she really was or not. Most people seemed to think she was a boy and she was tired of it.

Chan couldn't believe her eyes when Liu's uncle, arrived at their door one Sunday morning. He looked embarrassed. "I couldn't bear to see your disappointment when I had no money," he said. "That's why I didn't come these past three weeks. But today…" He handed Ma a fat envelope.

None of the younger boys were home so it was quiet but for the continuous beat of music everyone had grown so accustomed to no one noticed it anymore. Liu, Chan and Liu's uncle sat on the porch while Ma counted out two hundred Bahts. There was no note.

"I got a letter." Liu's uncle wiped foam from his upper lip after a long drink of the beer Ma had given him. "Your Father is very sad. He thought you were all dead. So many years of silence and only bad news from Cambodia. His new wife is angry and would not sign papers. I think she does not want you in America. I think maybe they had a big fight." He fiddled with his glass. "Your father is well thought of in Virginia Beach. Helps many Cambodians there. Think of him as a good man."

They sat in their own silence amid the incessant music and street sounds.

"He couldn't help it." Ma spoke quietly. "He is a man."

But Chan knew nothing of "men" only that he was her father whom she had believed in.

Now they had money for their journey Chan couldn't understand why no one was preparing to leave. They barely even mentioned it. It didn't seem fair to leave everything up to her. Were they all afraid of the outside world having been insulated in this camp for so long? Ma had changed since her heart problem; become quiet and slept a lot. Overwhelmed by the responsibility of having to arrange everything Chan thought of little else; transportation—and where would they stay once they reached Phnom Penh? Their flat was no longer theirs. Everyone they had known was gone. But they must leave this place! All these problems churned until she wanted to hide her head under a pillow.

"Don't worry, little Chan." Liu had come home late from work and now sat down beside her on the stoop where she had been looking at the stars, feeling small and helpless.

"You are not alone. I am here and will help you do whatever you want."

Something broke in Chan and she leaned her face into Liu's shoulder and wept until the tears stopped. He just stroked her head the whole time.

"Now, go to bed little one. Everything will be all right and as it should be."

She nodded, believing, and stumbled off to sleep.

Liu stayed sitting on the step and looking at the moon for a long while.

CHAPTER TWENTY-NINE

The imperious blast of a car's horn brought both Chanbopha and her mother to the door. It was early afternoon on a Monday. The two younger boys were at their English lesson. Vuthy and Sovirak had gone to get wood.

"Are you the Oum four people family?" An army officer climbed out of the land rover.

Both Chan and her mother nodded.

"Get your things. You are to leave for the U.S. now."

"Now?"

Ma said it. Chan's mouth just opened and shut.

"Quick. You are to leave immediately."

"Are you sure? Impossible!" Ma's head turned to right and left as though looking for truth.

Chan clung to Ma's arm. "You must give us time to bundle what we have. And the boys are away cutting wood. Please, sirs."

The younger officer looked at the other who, after a moment nodded. "Four o'clock then. We will be back at four." They drove away.

"We cannot go. Impossible. How can we trust those men? It is a trick". Ma was shaking, eyes fixed on the exhaust still whirling behind the vehicle.

"Ma, we are going to America! We must tell our friends. Gather our things. Say good-bye." Chanbopha heard her own words but couldn't believe them.

"Impossible!"

"Ma. We are going. In three hours. Papa must have sent for us. We are going to America." Each time Chan said it the fact became more real until she wanted to shout it over and over. Wanted to tell the whole camp. No horrible trip through Cambodia. No more boring days in this wretched place. No more music blaring day and night. No more of the bad smells they had all gotten used to! No more Liu...

For now he stood, looking down at her. "I will help you pack." His voice seemed unbearably sad.

News spread. Everyone they knew crowded into their house. Sovirak and Vuthy, when they got home, whooped for joy and joked about going to Hollywood and meeting movie stars. Even Liu's young brothers seemed sad to see them go. Ma had gotten over her distrust. If all these people believed their release was real it must be so. Amid tears Ma's shrine was dissembled and placed by the door. Chan looked at the small pile of their belongings. A bit more than they arrived with but not much.

"Chan. I have something to show you." It was Auntie Thuy who had assisted them in coming to the camp and who had verified the truth of Papa's new family. "Come, I don't want Ma to see this."

The two went out behind the house and there Auntie opened the newspaper she had been carrying.

In front of Chanbopha was a photograph of her father with the headline. "Tireless human rights advocate dangerously ill." She looked up at Auntie.

"That is why they are letting you go to him." Auntie took the paper and folded it as small as it would go. "Do not tell Ma. She is not strong enough to take any more shocks."

Chan nodded. Her mouth was dry, "Thank you, Auntie. You go back to the others. I'll wait here a moment."

Alone Chan went inside and sat at the table where she had eaten so many meals. There had been good times here. They had made friends. Many had left and more had arrived. She could hear voices now chattering on—saying how lucky the Oums were to be leaving.

Someone sat on the bench next to her. It was Liu and he just sat staring at the table in front of him.

"Liu?" said Chan.

He turned quickly and looked intently into her face. "I want to take care of you. I want to marry you." The words burst like birds from a cage. "You know I love you, Chanbopha."

And suddenly Chan did know and also knew she could not bear the thought of leaving him. But she must. "Oh Liu," she took his hand and pressed it against her cheek. "I am too young to talk of such things. My path is clear and I must think only of getting my family to America."

"I understand. But I will follow and find you there, my little Chan."

"Come, Daughter, they will be here any minute," Ma rushed in, pushing between them. "Have you got everything?"

At that moment the crowd went quiet as the Land Rover crept through to stop at the foot of the steps.

Then amidst sounds of laughing and crying, shouts wishing good luck and good-bye, Ma, Chan, the two boys and their belongings were hustled, lifted and shoved into the vehicle. The engine roared and they went hurtling down the street. Chan twisted to look back and saw Liu standing in the middle of the road his hand raised. She lifted her own, but too late, they turned a corner and he was gone. Something sank in her chest but she drew in a deep breath and looked ahead. We are going to America, she told herself. That's all that matters; all I want.

It was a bumpy, cramped ride to the small town of Chenberi, near Bangkok, where they were let off at a hotel especially for refugees. Chan wasn't hungry so when the others went down to eat in the hotel dining room she took out the newspaper Auntie had given her and read the article about her father more carefully. It was written by a friend of his named Joe, evidently a newspaper correspondent. Her father was portrayed as a hero to many people and in the accompanying photo he was giving a speech in front of a large crowd. He looked intense and dynamic and Chan was proud. Lastly was mentioned the strange illness he was hospitalized with. "Pray for his recovery," was the last line. It scared Chan, "Oh Papa," she whispered. "We're coming."

They remained in that little town for one week during which time Ma and Chan bought slacks to travel in and down jackets for the four of them in expectation of cold weather. They packed away the ID tags they had worn every day during the four previous years and for Chan it was as though a heavy weight was lifted from her. How strange to remember the relief she had felt when she first got hers.

On the morning of their departure Ma tied red ribbons around Chan's two shiny pony tails which she had never allowed to even be trimmed since leaving the prison camp. None of them could stomach breakfast. For Chan it was as much fear of spilling on her new clothes as lack of appetite. But soon her tummy was spinning with excitement as they boarded the huge silver plane and engines roared. Racing down the runway Chan felt Ma's fingernails dig into her wrist and knowing her mother was afraid made her own fear dissipate. She watched through the window next to her as, just clearing a row of trees, the plane lifted and the land grew smaller and farther away beneath them.

She let out the breath she hadn't known she was holding and looked around the now quiet cabin. Vuthy and Sovirak peered out their window, exclaiming about what they saw. Chan noted that the other passengers appeared to be refugees also. Everyone was happy, although they smiled with nervous eyes. A beautiful stewardess brought everyone soft drinks and small bags of peanuts and, later, meals in individual trays. She called Chan, "Cutie."

When Chan went to the small restroom she didn't flush for fear of it landing on someone's head down below. Perhaps they were only supposed to let it fall over the ocean.

Back in her seat she snuggled into the soft blanket the stewardess gave her. The engines throbbed. She felt disembodied—nowhere—between the past and the unknown future. For the moment free from decisions, Chanbopha slept.

CHAPTER THIRTY

It was February 28, 1987, twelve years after being driven out from Phnom Penh, when eighteen year old Chanbopha first looked down on the USA. It was all white. She had never seen snow before. A voice came over the intercom in both English and Chinese "We are about to land at New York John F. Kennedy airport. Due to the snow storm no more planes will be taking off today. United will place passengers in a hotel overnight. Tomorrow you will continue to your destination."

Chanbopha, jolted from imaginings of meeting her father and walking into their luxurious new home, groaned at this new delay.

"At least we will be able to clean up and look our best for Papa," said Ma.

Yes, thought Chan and feeling better she tightened her seat belt. Lights appeared through streaking snow; drew closer and closer and bigger. Her ears popped. Thump they were down, racing along the runway. Snow ceased being horizontal. The plane stopped and passengers filled the aisle, dragging luggage from overhead racks.

Too late Chan realized they needn't have spent those long hours with their carry-ons crammed in around them. She'd know next time.

"Better put on your jacket. It's cold out there." A smiling stewardess, thinking Chan didn't know English, mimicked the action and shivered.

Chan smiled back and followed the suggestion, passing it on to Ma and the boys. Then she was standing at the top of the steps looking across tarmac and breathing in the cold brisk air of America. She didn't care that her jacket, which seemed so heavy when she bought it, was like tissue against the wind. Snow flakes bit into her face like small piranha. She opened her mouth and let some fall onto her tongue. Someone pushed from behind and she jumped down the rest of the steps and almost danced her way to the building ahead. If only Liu were here to share this new world of lights and snow and big bustling people made bigger by their heavy clothes.

Warmth enveloped her as they entered a building where passengers were being hugged by people who had come to meet them.

"Move on," urged Ma, pushing Chan's shoulder. "Americans show feelings. Not like us. Don't stare."

"You must be the Oum family." A Chinese woman came up to them, smiling and speaking Khmer they could understand. What a relief that was! "I am Lily, a friend of your father and will help you settle in your hotel."

Chan looked about her at all the strange faces. "Where is my father?" she asked. "You are here. Why isn't he?"

"I am with the Cambodian Refugee Association here in New York City and our associates in Norfolk, when they learned of your unplanned stopover, phoned so I could help you. Tomorrow you fly to Norfolk. Come now."

The four of them followed as she, like the prow of an ice-ship, pushed her way through the crowd and out another door, back among the biting snowflakes. They headed toward a bus at the curb. "This will take you to the hotel. I dropped off overnight things on my way here. Your own luggage will be forwarded to Norfolk." Lily, stood aside as they boarded and found seats, then as they began to move away, she waved and shouted, "I will pick you up at eight tomorrow morning."

One minute too cold, the next too hot, thought Chanbopha, looking around at the other muffled up passengers who were loosening their scarves in the artificial heat. No wonder they all look so white. She leaned against the window fascinated by the sea of cars surrounding them as the bus merged into traffic. No bicycles or Tuk-Tuks. No cattle. No blaring horns. Just every make and color of shiny, new automobile. Even more amazing was how each kept in its own lane and obeyed traffic signals even while speeding on a road smoother than any she had seen before.

It seemed no time before the bus stopped and let them out at the door to a palace.

"It's a hotel," corrected Ma as they rushed through cold dusk into brightly lit heat which seemed to glow like the sun from every gilded surface. Tentatively Ma led the way up to the reception desk where a woman turned to them with a dazzling smile which made Chanbopha clench her lips tight over her own damaged teeth.

The woman handed out keys; one to Vuthy, one to Sovirak, one to Chan and the last to Ma. Each stood looking at the one they held.

"Take that elevator in the corner to the fourth floor and find your rooms. Necessary clothing is there for you and food has been ordered sent up. Be here in the lobby by seven thirty tomorrow morning and someone will take you to your plane." Her smile of dismissal grew even brighter.

"To Papa," thought Chan, wishing the receptionist wouldn't speak so fast.

The four Oums looked at each other then, keys tightly clutched, headed for the elevators.

Chan watched carefully as a man, obviously used to such things, pushed a large button which caused the doors to slide open. They all got inside and the doors closed. Chan felt a moment of fear as the box they were trapped in began to move.

It stopped and the doors opened. As the man began to leave, he paused. "What floor do you want?" he asked Ma.

She looked confused.

He smiled and looked at the key Chan held.

"Four," the man said, and pushed a button with a four on it. "Good luck," He stepped out and the Oums were shut back inside.

Chanbopha did not notice. She had made a horrifying discovery. Through all her years of studying English she had thought herself prepared for the United States. Now she realized she could understand only a smattering of words people spoke. It seemed that in spite of all her English classes she had learned to read and write but not to speak and understand. Americans spoke differently than her Asian teachers and much faster. She had told Papa she spoke English!

A soft jolt informed her the elevator had stopped. After a nerve wracking motionless moment the door silently slid open.

There was no sound from their feet on the carpeted hallway and no one spoke. 427 it said on Chan's key tag and when she opened the door to her room she gasped. Ahead soft lights bathed satin quilts on the two beds, heavy red drapes hid the window and the carpet was deeper than any bed she had slept on. She could see gleaming porcelain and tile through another open door and she wondered how many people in the hotel shared this one bathroom. Gold veined mirrors were everywhere and in all of them stood the same bewildered girl. She looked for Ma's image but it wasn't there.

She ran out into the hall and through the next open door saw Ma in the middle of a similar room. "Ma!" she called and at that moment Sovirak and Vuthy appeared and they all gathered together in a tight circle. "Please, Ma. I don't want to sleep alone in that big room," said Chan. None of them had ever slept alone.

"Everything okay?" A plump woman stood in the doorway, penciled eyebrows raised higher than was natural. Chan grabbed the two keys the boys held and forced them into the woman's hands. She was quick to understand their wish for only two of the rooms and her eyes went warm. She said something Chan didn't understand, then with a smile trundled on down the hall pushing her cart of mops and clean towels.

Without a word the boys moved into Ma's room and Ma returned with Chan to 427. The mirrors reflected the two of them as they pinched the fine blankets and soft sheets, exclaimed over the towels and lotions in the bathroom and flushed the amazing toilet. What a wealthy country this was!

A waiter appeared with food and the boys joined Ma and Chan for the fine Chinese meal Lily had ordered. After that they opened the bags of clothes Lily had left for them. Most everything was too large for Chan but with Ma's help they made things fit by folding pant legs and sleeves of the smallest sized jackets and trousers until Chan was pleased with her appearance in the mirror. There was a red knit cap which did fit perfectly and she hoped Papa would like it. But would he recognize her? Ma and the boys looked strange in American winter clothes and for a moment Chan had a strange panicky feeling as if she were losing everything familiar. Losing her own self. Leaving Liu far behind.

"I'm going to have a shower." She went into the bathroom, shut the door and stripped off the new clothes. In the mirror she was herself again. She tore plastic from the new red tooth brush, turned on the taps over the sink and scrubbed her teeth with toothpaste from the miniature tube. Poor teeth so disfigured from eating all that hard rice in the Pol Pot's rice paddies. There was another brush there for Ma. Chan unwrapped the sweet smelling soaps. So many towels, and hair shampoos and lotions. She wanted to collect them all to take with her.

The shower lurked behind a cloudy glass door. Chan removed her underclothes and tiptoed inside. She turned a knob then leaped out with a yelp as scalding water struck her. The boys and Ma rushed in. "What happened? Are you all right?" The room was rapidly filling with steam. "Turn it off!" shrieked Chan. Sovirak turned a lever and everything stopped.

"You turned the hot," he accused and reached for another lever. This time it gushed icy cold, soaking his head and new jacket. Vuthy jumped in to turn it off but this time a fine spray filled the stall. Ma shouted to shut the door as the whole bathroom was getting soaked. Everyone was wet now and each person thought they knew the magic to control this out of control water. So many buttons and levers and ways to turn the showerhead. Among the four of them they must have tried them all.

Chan began to laugh and it spread until they all collapsed onto the tiles under the steady warm stream of their last experiment. Chan pointed to their sodden images in the mirrored ceiling and that made them laugh even harder.

Loud hammering on the door quieted them. Ma opened it to the enquiring face of the housekeeper they had seen before. She took one look around and beckoned to Ma. They all crowded close as she demonstrated the machinations of modern plumbing: turn knob toward green for cold, the red dot for hot, twist small lever on the nozzle for heavy spray or mist and so on. Then she handed each person a clean towel, gave them a wide grin and left.

The boys and Ma left Chanbopha with the shower set to a comfortable temperature and she stood for a long time luxuriating in the unending water that poured onto the top of her head and down her body. She unwrapped a bar of soap and scrubbed herself all over, including her hair, then rinsed and rinsed. When she finally stepped out onto a soft mat and dried herself with a huge fluffy towel she had never felt so clean. She wished she could tell Liu about it and how they had all laughed. She felt a wave of sadness, thinking of him back there still in that hot, noisy refugee camp. But that quickly passed as she thought of how, by this time tomorrow, she would be with Papa.

Chan's bed was so soft she feared she would sink out of sight so she spent most of the night sleeping soundly, wrapped in blankets on the floor. Ma seemed comfortable, to judge from her snores, which to Chan were comforting in this strange place.

Lily arrived early next morning with doughnuts and coffee. "Popular American breakfast," she explained. They were all dressed in the clothes she had provided and she looked them up and down approvingly. "Come, eat up. It will soon be time to leave for the plane to Norfolk, Virginia."

Chanbopha ate three of the delicious American donuts, immediately felt ill, and prayed she wouldn't disgrace herself by throwing up.

Lily's exhortations for them to get ready to leave took her mind off that and instead she asked, "Will Papa recognize me in my new hat?" But Lily just whisked them into the elevator and then onto the bus and through the airport.

One short flight and then would begin her new life in that beautiful house with Papa. Chanbopha completely forgot about her upset stomach and to say goodbye to Lily.

Chan became oblivious to everything but the white clouds they passed through and the white countryside beneath. She couldn't wait to land but was scared too. She smoothed her hair ribbons and, looking at her reflection in the window, adjusted her cap to just above where her fringe ended.

"We are about to land at Norfolk airport. Do not release your seat..."

Chan's mouth was dry. She caught Ma's eye and received a tremulous smile. She hadn't thought about how she must feel about meeting her husband after twelve years apart.

From the top of the plane's steps Chan looked for her father among the small crowd by the entrance to the building. Her head kept turning, eyes searching as they walked across the pavement. Where was he?

Two women stepped forward. One asked in Khmer, "You are the Oum family?"

Ma said yes but Chan was on tiptoes looking over the woman's shoulder. "Papa? Where is my father?"

"I am the social worker," said the one who looked Cambodian and kind, "And Ting is here with me to translate for

Mrs…" she paused an embarrassed moment, "aaah-Karly, who is here to welcome you."

A blond American woman trotted up, puffing, and shook hands with each of the family. Her smile was made only of lipstick.

CHAPTER THIRTY-ONE

Chanbopha was looking everywhere in the waiting room they had entered as if her father might be hiding in a corner somewhere.

"Where is Papa?" she repeated over and over.

The interpreter looked down at the floor and spoke slowly prompted by the American. "Do not worry about your father. We are here instead of him."

Chan interrupted. "You don't understand. This a special day for us."

The American spoke sharply and the translator said, "He's busy."

"Not too busy to meet us! Where is he?"

After a pause the woman said, "He's sick. In hospital."

Of course. How could I have forgotten, thought Chan. "Take us to him. To the hospital!" she demanded bolting toward the door but the Social worker stopped her. "No!"

"First we must get your luggage, then lunch before discussing the situation." The Social worker set off to where Chan saw their belongings revolving with other passenger's suitcases in the middle of the room. The American woman said something and left with the interpreter. Only then did Chan realize that she must have been Pa's new wife.

Reunited with their bags they were taken to the cafeteria and bought a lunch of unfamiliar food neither Ma nor Chan could eat, although Sovirak and Vuthy devoured theirs. Chan was tense like a tiger in a cage. Ma seemed confused and close to panic. Finally, unable to bear the suspense, Chan blurted, "Now tell us!"

The social worker shrugged and looked down at the table in front of her. "Michael Odom passed away three days ago."

"Who?" asked Vuthy.

"I guess no one told you but your father changed his name. Here he was Michael Odom."

Stunned silence.

"Your father died two days ago," she repeated. "They say of hepatitis."

Chan stopped breathing. Ma collapsed against Vuthy's shoulder. Sovirak leaped to his feet and stared at the social worker who muttered over and over, "I'm so sorry!" She handed out Kleenex to the boys, who had tears pouring down their cheeks. Chanbopha was too shocked to do anything.

Someone had called an ambulance and Chan watched as big men loaded Ma onto a stretcher and took her away. Chan gulped a great choking sob and desperately hung on to her brothers while the social worker fluttered around trying to calm everyone as she herded them outside and into a taxi.

A short ride and they were taken into an apartment occupied by a Cambodian couple. It smelled of babies and cooking.

"These are good people whom your father helped." explained the Social worker. "Now they help you. A car will come for you tomorrow morning." She left.

Chan looked down into the brown eyed faces of four small children.

"I made tea," said their mother. "You may have this sitting room. It is a small apartment but warm. The bathroom is down the hall. I am very sorry." And she backed out, hustling her children with her.

Chanbopha sat on the sofa between Sovirak and Vuthy. She felt as though her world had dissolved under her feet leaving her naked in a cold wind with nowhere to turn. This must be a nightmare she thought—tomorrow I will wake up and Papa will be here.

She awoke to find herself on the sofa covered by a blanket while Sovirak and Vuthy slumped under similar covers in the two armchairs. All were still in the clothes they had worn yesterday and looked rumpled and confused. Gratefully they accepted the strong tea and rice their hostess gave them. She stayed while they ate, and told of many wonderful things Papa had done for the Cambodian community and her family in particular. She also said how everyone disliked the woman he had married. "She didn't want him to help us. Didn't like him spending money she expected for the three children of her first husband. I heard that man killed himself."

"Her first husband died too?" Chan asked.

At that moment a yellow taxi arrived out front. Chan was relieved to see her mother in the rear seat and ran to join her; the boys followed. Instead of the woman from the day before a man sat in front next to the driver. He introduced himself as Joe, father's best friend. "We met when I was writing a story on his work with the Cambodian refugees here. I'm a newspaper reporter."

"I read a story you wrote. About Pa being sick and doing good things," said Chan, feeling the relief of a connection to this man.

He spoke understandable Khmer and Chan wondered if her father had taught him. She liked his kind smile and understanding eyes.

"You are taking us to see my father?" she asked.

"I am taking you to the hospital—to see papers. His American wife does not want you to see him."

Chan leaned forward. "I want to see my father. I will see my father!"

Her voice high and panicky brought their hosts of last night close and several Cambodian neighbors. When they heard the story they all began to talk at once, telling Joe how necessary it was for a Cambodian man's family to say farewell to his body.

Chan saw that Joe understood and at last he shrugged and gave different orders to the driver who already had the engine running.

It was a short drive to the funeral home. They pushed through the heavy door into a room thick with quiet. All Chan heard was the roar of her own blood. Joe whispered to the solemn, black suited man behind the desk and they were seated in black throne-like, maroon cushioned chairs to wait for the body to be wheeled out for viewing. Shortly the man stood and beckoned them to follow through a door into an even quieter, smaller room. In the middle, on a raised dais, stood an ornate box and Chan knew Papa was in it. But maybe not. Maybe Michael Odom was not Captain Oum at all! Perhaps it held the wrong man! This hope lasted until she reached the casket and, standing on tiptoe, looked down on Papa's face. In spite of the surprising amount of makeup, or perhaps because of it, he looked the same as she remembered so long ago. "Papa," Chan whispered. "Papa, we are here. Your family! Wake up!"

But that still, peaceful face never moved.

On impulse Chan leaned in. Hugged the still chest. Pressed her tear-wet face to his cold cheek. His ear, stiff as plastic, scratched her skin. "Papa. Why do you go away? Who can we depend on? Wake up! We have no home! No Money! We cannot survive without you! Oh Papa…"

Joe gently pulled her away as she still reached out to that last vestige of what had been her driving force and goal for almost as long as she could remember.

Tears blinded her to Ma and her brothers' farewell to the soldier husband and father, and she barely noticed the ride back to the apartment where they sat numbly while people came and went offering comfort with words and food.

As Chanbopha washed before bed she looked a second time at her face in the mirror; at the livid scratch on her temple then the tan color on her white washcloth. It could only have come from Papa. Why had the funeral home done all that makeup? And why so much?

CHAPTER THIRTY-TWO

The next few days passed in a daze while life surged around Chanbopha in that crowded apartment.

"You must dress your best." It was Joe on the phone. "Your father's wife is giving a celebration of his life at her house this afternoon. Everyone's invited. I've asked a wonderful lady, Sony, to come to help you get ready and take you to the event."

So, at last we will see the house and meet Papa's second family, thought Chan, and the idea rallied her from her doldrums. She encouraged her brothers to shower and clean up. "We must make a good impression. Show what a fine family Papa has."

When the woman called Sony arrived they were all in their cleanest clothes but she had brought new looking jackets and trousers for the boys, and dresses for Ma and Chan. They all loved Sony immediately, so bubbly and encouraging, and for moments forgot their plight in the excitement of seeing the change in each other.

Sovirak and Vuthy, hair slicked down and in their new outfits, looked like grown men. Ma was elegant in an ankle length black dress with a high collar.

"I'm lending you these," said Sony fastening pearls around Ma's neck then standing back. "You look like a queen," she beamed.

And she did, thought Chan, seeing her mother as she remembered her long ago so regal with her hair coiled on top of her head.

"Now you, Chanbopha. You will be the princess."

"I think this dress is too short," Chan felt shy looking in the mirror. She had almost lived in shorts but this deep blue dress so far above her knees was different.

Sony laughed. "It is perfect; the fashion for teenagers. Now I shall comb your lovely long hair over your shoulders and add this as a gift from me." She fastened a gold locket on a long chain around Chan's neck. "And you can find a good photo of your Papa to put inside it."

Chan couldn't believe the girl in the mirror was herself; the scrawny, half starved prison camp survivor and refugee. She looked modern and... and well... beautiful! If only Papa could see her—and Liu. He would be so surprised!

"Don't forget these," Sony was saying, holding out a box. "Hope they fit."

Carefully Chan removed the lid. "Oh my!" she breathed, "Look Ma, shoes with the high heels behind!"

"Not very high," corrected Sony laughing. "We don't want broken ankles! Put them on. Now we must go."

It was a strange feeling for Chanbopha as their taxi pulled up in front of the house she had so often envisioned—but in much different circumstances. Her legs almost refused to carry her up the walkway and, although her family and Sony were around her, Chan felt very alone as she faced the woman waiting to greet them. They had briefly met at the airport but everything there had been too confusing to register.

Chan was enveloped in a cloud of perfume, then appraised by eyes screened behind thickly mascara'd lashes. Jewels dangled from ears, neck and wrists while Chan's fingers were bruised by her handshake armored with rings.

"And you must be my dear husband's family from so long ago," the voice was syrupy with a nasal twang. "Come in and see my house. My daughter will show you around."

A gangly young girl came over, obviously annoyed, muttered a curt hello, and led the way through rooms Chan already knew from photographs. But she had imagined them as her home, not like this, and it made a frightening confusion in her mind.

The girl largely ignored the Oum family but chatted animatedly to Sony who passed on relevant information. "She says this was her father's bedroom," Sony said at the door to a small spartan room.

But he was not legally your father, thought Chan, noting that this girl must be no younger than twelve years old.

"And this is my mother's." She flung open another door, and seeming bored with the whole thing, moved on down the hall. The boys followed her but Ma and Chan stayed looking in at the room which glowed pink. Roses adorned heavy drapes which touched thick wine-red rugs. A pink shimmering bedspread covered a huge round bed and a bowl of roses wilted on a dresser beside a gold mirror and brush set. No sign of Papa's presence here.

Sony had come back for them.

"My husband and the lady did not sleep in the same room?" said Ma, and Chan thought she detected a note of pleasure in her voice.

Sony put her finger to her lips, "I asked the girl about that. She answered, not since he learned you were alive. You know Mrs. Oum, your husband felt very terrible. He was a good man, a very good man. But his American wife was angry. Was afraid you would take all this away from her and her children. She made things very bad for him. Come now."

They joined the guests. "Well, did you like my house?" Pa's second wife, who in Cambodia would be called Kantima, asked loudly, leaving no room for answer. "Now meet my other children."

The two young men must have been almost twenty and barely spared a nod toward the Oums who tried to reply. "Sorry I don't understand a word you people say," said the oldest and both walked away with sour expressions on their faces.

"Come over here, there's food," called Vuthy.

As they sampled the many dishes on the long table Cambodians whom Papa had helped came and expressed sympathy for their loss. These people all obviously disliked their hostess. "She big show off always. So many cars and jewelry. She brags he leave so much money from his Real Estate business."

Someone else chimed in. "I think that money some he raise to help new Cambodians. Now she take it all."

"They say Mr. Odom died of hepatitis but I hear he burned in fire accident at hospital."

"Shhh, here she comes."

But Chanbopha was remembering the makeup on the side of her face after hugging Papa at the funeral home-and the scratch from his perhaps artificial ear if he'd been burned. Poor Papa!

People wandered off and began to leave. Vuthy and Sovirak tidied away chairs while Ma and Chan loaded dishes into a dish washer. They had never seen such a thing before and Chan wondered why she was told to wash everything before putting it in the machine if it was supposed to be that useful. Papa's second wife ordered them about as though they were servants and all the time bragged about the cost of the tableware, the artwork on the walls, the highly polished furniture and Persian rugs. Then she moved on to how brilliant her children were and the expensive schools they attended. "By the way, they said they couldn't talk to you. That you don't know English. My husband said you told him you learned it in that camp place you were in."

Chan began to explain but the woman broke in bemoaning the fact that her plans for a trip to Hawaii had to be cancelled because of "all this."

Chan just happened, at that moment, to let a crystal goblet slip from her fingers to smash into gleaming shards on the floor.

"Time to go home," Sony burst into the kitchen. "We all need sleep. Big day tomorrow with the funeral and all!" She whisked them into their coats, then out into the cold where a car already purred, warm and waiting with Joe at the wheel. Papa's second wife and children paid no attention to their leaving.

"Your Papa had a good business. There should be money for you," Sony murmured. "But she's clever, that one."

The ride back to the apartment seemed long and Chan looked out of the car window but recognized nothing. They seemed to be in a better part of town than she had seen before and the faces were all white.

She turned a puzzled look on Sony who smiled. "Oh, I forgot to mention, you are coming to stay with me, My apartment is big and I am alone. We have your belongings in the trunk. The other place is too crowded and was a hardship for the family although they were happy to help you."

How kind everyone is, thought Chan, I shall repay them some day.

CHAPTER THIRTY-THREE

The smell of wet earth and sodden coats seemed as unreal as the droning of the minister's voice to Chanbopha as she huddled with Ma and her brothers, grieving and chilled to the bone. They had had no white clothing, which is the custom for funerals in Cambodia but Sony had found four white scarves for them to wear and that made them feel a little better. Ma was especially upset about Pa having a Christian burial rather than the proper Buddhist cremation but, as Sony said, his American wife had the authority to do what she wanted.

The subdued crowd mumbled Amens and the second wife and her three children slumped under oversized black umbrellas close to the hole into which Papa's coffin was being lowered. Chanbopha had to keep shifting position to see past the people in front of her whom she suspected were the second wife's relatives.

Tears mixed with rain on Chan's cheeks as earth was thrown onto the casket. Thud. Thud. Each thud sounded like another "gone." On and on until she had to stop it.

'Papa!" she wailed pushing her way to the front and only Sovirak's strong hands on her shoulders held her from flinging herself into that rapidly filling cavity.

It was then that Chan noticed the two head stones on adjoining plots. The first was engraved with the second wife's name, the final date left blank. The other bore a man's name-the final date filled in. Her first husband? How terrible for Papa to be buried next to that stranger, without even a headstone of his own!

The new grave had become a pile of wet soil. People were leaving. She darted after Second wife. "They made a mistake. They forgot Papa's stone. No one will be able to find him!"

Someone translated as Kantina jerked her arm away from Chan's reach. "Foolish girl, headstones are put up later, not at the funeral. Besides I have already paid for two, I cannot afford another."

"But…"

"If you want one you buy it. He was a bad husband to me but I got the last word and I hope he knows it!"

She tottered off across the lawn, high heels sinking into the turf as her words were translated for Chan who shouted after her in her own Khmer language, "Some day I will buy him a better stone than yours! You'll see!"

Chan didn't care that the woman did not know Khmer but from the look she bestowed before getting into her car Chan guessed she understood enough.

Ma looked shocked and a chatter of clapping came from the few Cambodians still there. Sovirak and Vuthy stood on either side of Chan as she bent and patted the fresh grave. "I will Papa. I promise." And as the rain pelted harder they all ran to the car.

CHAPTER THIRTY-FOUR

The following days were spent exploring the area where they lived. Sony was away working in her Real Estate office so Chan and her mother spent the mornings making the apartment as spotless as possible, then the four of them walked the nearby streets afraid of going too far lest they never find their way back.

After Sony returned from work and had eaten the dinner Ma prepared, she drove them around town explaining and pointing things out as she laughed at their reactions. She took them to a mall where Chan was overwhelmed by the noise, music and colors. Stores sold things she had never heard of but the abundance frightened her and she was glad to leave.

Sony took them into their first supermarket and they exclaimed in amazement at the colorful array of foods. Chan and her brothers wandered up the produce aisle stopping to admire the great variety of vegetables, all so clean it was hard to imagine they had grown in soil.

Srey with her fetish for cleanliness would have liked America Chan thought, feeling a wave of sadness for the little sister she had almost forgotten.

As Vuthy leaned to look and argue over the name of something that looked like a carrot but wasn't orange, a low growl preceded a sudden downpour and rumble of thunder. Vuthy leaped back, his hair soaked.

"Vuthy, what have you done!" squealed Chanbopha, looking around for the manager who must surely be on his way to reprimand them.

Vuthy appeared ready to run but Sovirak stopped him.

Chanbopha, close to tears, longed for the arrival of Sony who had stopped in another aisle. She could not bear to have her brother put in jail after all they had been through. Then she noticed other shoppers smiling at them. The water had stopped. No angry manager appeared. Nothing seemed damaged.

"Ready to go?" Sony appeared pushing her full shopping cart and they all followed her through checkout and back to the car.

Chan noticed Vuthy smoothing down his hair as the three of them gave half smiles to each other.

They never told either Ma or Sony about the scare in the store but it taught them that anything could happen in America.

The boys got small jobs unpacking newly arrived items for different stores mostly owned by Cambodian immigrants. The day when they came home with their first American paycheck everyone whooped for joy and they all hugged, but Chan knew they needed much more to make it in this big rich country. First they needed a plan but she could not think of one and it kept her awake at night staring at the strange ceiling that was not her father's as in all those previous dreams of only a month before.

The boys had no sooner left on another snowy Tuesday than they were back again, bursting through the door waving a newspaper in their mother and sister's faces.

"Read it! Read it!" Sovirak shouted, "It's about us. Even a photograph!"

They smoothed the paper open on the table and at first Chan barely recognized the four people in their unfamiliar clothes, looking wild eyed into the camera. It had been taken when they first arrived at the airport. Next to it was a photo of Papa looking like an American business man. At least they could all read English, so Vuthy began to read the story aloud. It was mainly about how Mr. Odom, who worked in real estate and championed the Cambodian immigrants in Myrtle Beach and vicinity, had long ago given up hope that his own family in Cambodia could still be alive. "Surely they had been among the two million Cambodians slaughtered during the Pol Pot genocide," Vuthy stopped reading and looked at the others in horror. "Two million dead?"

"Two million!" The others mouthed back.

"Some say three million," Ma said quietly. "Even babies. Sony told me."

"I saw…" Chanbopha's whisper trailed off as she pushed back the memories trying to escape from that dark corner of her mind where she hid them.

Sovirak took over reading, "The surviving family of four finally got to America after suffering years as prisoners and refugees, only to find that Michael Odom, their father, had died just days before their arrival.

Now this brave, grieving family is stranded, destitute, not knowing what to do. So ironic such a predicament should occur to the wife and children of a man who has helped so many Cambodian refugees attain good lives in this land of opportunity."

Chan added, "Father's friend, Joe, wrote it."

They each took turns silently reading it again. Chan didn't know whether she felt embarrassed at having their lives spread out before everyone or excited to see her family in the news just like important people. There was more about the poor, grieving American widow, who also thought her husband's first family was dead, but Chan didn't want to read about her.

When Sony came home that evening she also brought a paper—this time the New York Times—with almost the same story although some names were spelled differently and events changed.

Two days later when Joe came by, the Oums surrounded him exclaiming about the article he had written.

"But look!" Papa's tall American friend pushed his way past them to the table and dumped the contents of his brief case on its shiny surface. Dozens of white envelopes piled into a mountain, all addressed to the Oums.

"What is this?" whispered Chan.

"Open one, "said Joe.

They all looked toward Ma who hesitantly stepped forward. Joe handed her an envelope. The flap was already unstuck and she drew out a check. "One hundred dollars." she murmured. "For us," as she read "Oum family" on the 'pay to' line. "Why?" she asked looking up at Joe.

"People loved your father and others felt sad to read your story. It touched their hearts and they want to help. All these envelopes contain checks for you."

Chan filled to the brim with emotion. She hadn't even confessed to herself how frightened she had been. How desolate their future appeared. And how, in a way, she blamed herself for landing them in this predicament.

Tears stung and she noticed everyone else had unusually shiny eyes. Even Joe. She hugged him, squeezing so hard his coat buttons dug into her cheek. "How can I thank them all? And you?"

"I will thank them for you through the paper. And I am happy to help my good friend's wonderful family."

For several weeks donations poured in. Sony took Ma to the bank and opened a checking account—showing her how to use it—and Ma came home with an extra bounce to her step. Excitedly she showed her children the little book with the large amount of dollars marked down in it. More were added every day.

CHAPTER THIRTY-FIVE

Sony called a meeting. She had just returned from work at Father's real estate office and the boys had washed up after a hard day of unloading furniture into an office building.

"Before we eat I want to talk. Today I saw the first crocus poking through the snow. Spring will come soon. Winter vacation is ending and school begins. You can afford to rent your own apartment now and I have found a good one in a suburb called Hampton. I have arranged for Chanbopha, Vuthy and Sovirak to attend the nearby high school. You can go there because you have an American father."

This surprised Chan. She had never thought he might have acquired citizenship!

"There will be no cost. Also, you will receive money each month from your father's Social Security. You will all have to work after school but you will be independent and on your way!" Sony smiled around at them.

Could all this really be true! Those last words especially thrilled Chan and also knowing she was signed up for school. She knew that education was the way to a good life, the belief having been impressed on her so long ago by Pa when he was teaching economics at Phnom Penh University.

They didn't have many possessions so the move was easy. When Sony left them in their new apartment that first Saturday Chan was almost afraid to move lest she break the spell and wake up back in some crowded hut. She dug her toes into the soft carpet. The boys were turning water on and off in the bathroom, shouting to each other. Ma was in the kitchen inspecting the stove and when she let out a yelp Chan ran in to see. Ma had opened the fridge and found it filled with all their favorite foods.

"Sony," murmured Chan.

Her mother just nodded.

There were three bedrooms—Vuthy and Sovirak each had one for himself while Chanbopha still shared a room with Ma although they had twin beds. That night, as she lay cozy under warm blankets Chan wondered where Liu was. She imagined him still in the camp, pedaling every day to the embassy, still living on those meager rations. She wished she could tell him she was about to go to a real American school. Would he care? He may not even remember her. Sometimes it was hard to know which life was reality and which the dream. Often cruel faces haunted her nights, or a blast of music from a passing car took her back to the refugee camp. The scream of a child playing could make her blood go cold or a smell remind her of death. Sometimes it was hard to eat the food in front of her although it was good and she was hungry. She didn't understand.

Sony came to accompany her and the boys to school on Monday. They took a bus, as they must do alone in future, and Sony led them through the big doors and down halls filled with shouting, shoving boys and girls who looked like giants to small Chanbopha. But she was too excited to be afraid, and thrilled when introduced to her teacher who assigned her a desk near the front of the room. Chan didn't admit how little spoken English she knew but as classes commenced she could read whatever was written on the blackboard or in books which were handed out and no one seemed to care that she hardly spoke.

At lunchtime she found Vuthy and Sovirak who had not fared as well.

Everyone had laughed whenever they made a mistake and their science teacher had become impatient and sharply corrected them several times. But they didn't seem to mind and as both were good at math they had earned respect when it came time for that class.

They shared their experiences as they sat together eating the sandwiches Ma had made and though they were given curious glances no student spoke to them.

After school the boys caught a bus to look for work downtown so Chan had to go home alone. She was jubilant. She had learned many new things and the teacher turned out to be very kind and filled Chan's back pack, a gift from Sony, with books studied the term before so she could catch up. Other students milled around the bus stop and pushed her aside when the bus arrived. At first she gave way to them then she put her elbows to work and set out to prove she could also be tough.

She had only just battled her way on board when with a jolt the bus started off.

Too late Chan reached for a handhold and the weight of her backpack hurled her to her knees. She could hear laughter as she struggled to stand. No one offered to help. One knee bled, spattering her new shoes. She pretended not to notice and not to care that there was nowhere left for her to sit. She clung to a seatback and was enormously relieved when the bus driver called out her stop. Ignoring everyone, head high, she left without stumbling and trudged to the apartment and up the stairs, hating the backpack she had been so proud of that morning.

Nobody was home. First she cleaned the blood off her shoe, then she sat down and studied the day's lesson which was not at all difficult now she had time to think. After a drink of tea she looked through the books the teacher had given her, wishing she could in one gulp swallow all the knowledge between their covers.

She didn't tell Ma about the incident on the bus nor how the other students had ignored her or laughed at her English when she spoke. She did tell how nice the teacher was and could see how happy and relieved Ma was to hear it. Then and there Chan assigned herself to make at least one friend soon and to show everyone in class that just because she came from another country, was smaller than they were and spoke little English, she was just as smart—maybe even smarter than many of them.

Next day on the bus, with a lightened backpack and armed with resolve, she looked into the grinning faces of some boys who leaned over from the seat in front of hers.

"You no speakee English," mocked one as his buddies laughed.

Chan stared daggers into his eyes. "Better than you speak Khmer." she snapped back.

Kids nearby laughed but this time at the boy, who turned to face front.

Chan noticed how red his ears were and felt empowered. She would be okay. Now to find a friend. And not a Cambodian. Only from being with Americans would she learn to speak well and become a good American.

The first class that day was called PE. Chanbopha didn't know what that meant and after roll call watched as everyone left the room except the teacher, who was concentrating on some papers. She was a different one from yesterday. Chan cleared her throat and the woman looked up, eyebrows raised.

"I don't know what to do," Chan said, feeling stupid and lost.

"PE. Just follow the others to the locker room." The teacher waved toward the door and returned to her work.

Chan went out into the hall and stood there in the hollow emptiness. For so long, in fact for most of her life, she had lived in a world where every moment was crowded with people and noise. She had learned to shut it all out. Now this silence seemed more intrusive, and she strained to hear something, anything. Even alone in the jungle there had been sounds: birds, insects, monkeys, bullhorn from the nearby camp.

A girl appeared from the other direction and ran through a door releasing a burst of voices. Then all was quiet again.

Chan went to where she had disappeared and tentatively pushed. Teacher was wrong, this was not a locked room at all.

She entered and stood amazed. Girls were everywhere, in various stages of undress. Some entirely naked. What was going on! She fled into the hall and back to the safety of the classroom.

Teacher looked up, frowning.

"The locked room was not locked. Girls were taking off clothes. I don't understand."

The woman smiled and came around to the front of her desk. "Poor little Chan. Of course you wouldn't know. That is a locker room. Not a locked room. And a locker is a place where each student can keep belongings. There is one for you there too." She looked down at a paper on the desk behind her. "Number 69 is yours. You put your own code in your lock, then only you can get in. Keep your exercise clothes there."

Chanbopha nodded as though she understood.

The teacher returned to her papers and Chan went back into the hall. She recognized classmates exiting the locker room, and studied their clothes; shorts, white t-shirts and white gym shoes. She would borrow money from the fund to buy the same for herself.

She didn't go into the gym but sat on a bench outside, shivering. After what seemed a painfully long time the door banged open and the girls poured out and streamed back to the locker room. Chan waited and joined them to reenter the class room with the boys who must have had PE elsewhere.

She felt comfortable during the lessons, was good in math, and concentrated in other subjects where she could often get the meaning of spoken sentences by guessing from the few words she did recognize. Everyone was surprised that she could read and write English so well.

"We had school in refugee camp. I received high school certificate but no American teachers there for us to hear and talk," she explained.

She noticed people treating her differently after that. More like a person than a bug they had looked down on. But she still needed a friend.

Her chance came one afternoon as she left the schoolyard and saw a classmate bent over the bicycle she rode to school every day.

"You need help?" asked Chan.

"Oh, I'll just have to push it home. The stupid chain's come off."

"I put on for you." Chan set her backpack on the pavement and crouched down beside the crippled machine. Her fingers remembered all the times she had helped Liu with his bike's chain which was always slipping. What was he doing now? She tried not to remember him standing in the road waving as she left.

"Hey, you've done it! Thanks tons! My name's Robin, what's yours?"

"Chan," Chanbopha took the proffered hand and inwardly rejoiced—she had a friend.

The next morning Robin helped Chan set the code on locker 69 and Chan locked new white gym shoes, shorts and t-shirt safely inside.

Robin's friends now welcomed Chan to join them for lunch in the school dining room and due to going to ESL classes at night the whole Oum family was feeling more confident. However the only money coming in was what Ma earned picking crabs with other Cambodians at the big factory downtown, and the boys' odd jobs on weekends, so Chan felt guilty whenever she bought something for school—especially the white gym shoes.

She had mentioned this worry to Sony who often visited and when she arrived one day in the middle of the week it was with news. "I hear the Chinese restaurant Lotus Flower down the way needs a busboy. I signed you up. Just weekends. You'll get minimum wage but it's something. You start this Saturday. They expect you at four o'clock. Isn't that wonderful?" Sony, smiling. spread her fingers wide. "No more guilt."

Chan dutifully thanked her then, "Sony, but what is a busboy?"

Sony explained the part about clearing tables but didn't seem clear about what else.

And act like a boy Chan concluded to herself. She could do anything: hadn't she told herself that since she could remember?

CHAPTER THIRTY-SIX

"You too puny and weak." The Chinese manager at Lotus Flower eyed Chan up and down. "You no good busboy. You go home to Mama."

Chan, after a morning of homework, had walked the eight long blocks and then up and down looking for the restaurant. She was hot, despite the cold spring wind, and her feet hurt in the new shoes bought for the new job. She found the place at exactly four o'clock and now, facing the manager she was not going to be fired before even starting.

"I am very strong," said Chan. "Let me show you."

Customers were pouring in. "Okay." said Mr. Chu as his name tag proclaimed. "Only half wage then. Go to kitchen. Cook will tell you what to do." He bowed to an American couple and greeted them by name.

Chan slipped behind him and ran to the back of the dining room where waiters were coming and going through a swinging door. She saw a table with empty dishes and took them into the kitchen. By watching she understood her job and smiled at the customers as she poured their water or brought them spring rolls their waitress had forgotten.

The last customer left at eleven thirty. Chan lined up with the other employees, none of whom had spared her a word or glance all evening. Chan guessed they were all part of the same Chinese family and they didn't like outsiders. Each was given an envelope with their evening's pay. No envelope fell into her hands. "Uncle?" she whispered.

He stopped and looked at her.

"My pay?" she whispered.

"You learner. No pay yet," he said and moved on to the next employee who received a fat envelope and smirked sideways at Chanbopha as she flaunted crisp new bills.

Chan felt miserable on the long walk home through cold darkness. Everyone was in bed when she got there and she was glad she didn't have to tell Ma of her humiliation and disappointment at not being able to leave money on the kitchen table as she had imagined.

Every weekend Chan walked to the restaurant, arriving early and leaving late, doing extra chores-but the Chinese never thanked her, only shouted, and treated her like a slave.

Finally she received pay. Ninety nine cents an hour. Tips were shared among all the workers but she only got half what they did.

"Why I get less?" She confronted the manager who was greeting patrons at the door with his ingratiating smile. "You see I work hard. Do more than the others."

He looked down his Chinese nose at her. "But you have little English." He turned away, "Good evening Mr. and Mrs. Jenkins! Your usual table?"

"How is Lotus Flower?" asked Ma one evening.

Chan knew how hard Ma worked and refused to burden her mother further. "Okay. But not a good place. No choice until I have good English. I must be patient and study hard."

She had one friend at the restaurant, the Cambodian Chef. He and his family lived in the same apartment building as the Oums and having read about their plight he sympathized with Chan. Often they walked home together which was comforting through late night streets. She could talk to him of her frustration at work but never hinted of it at home. They were all too tired from their own daily struggles.

"The library is good place to learn," Chef advised. "To speak English well is most important for your future."

So Chan spent every free hour at the local library which the bus passed to and from school. Her slight frame, big eyes and earnest questions endeared her to the librarian who spent free time coaching her and lending her helpful books. She even gave Chanbopha a small tape recorder and some English as a Second Language tapes which Chan played late at night in her room, repeating exercises in a whisper until Ma complained. She also watched American soap operas on the small TV Joe gave them as a Christmas gift and listened to American radio talk shows. Soon she was speaking out in class and everyone understood. No one made fun of her anymore.

Then a wonderful thing happened. It was at the library, in her ESL class when just before the break the teacher set something strange in front of Chan. She stared at the heavily iced cupcake adorned with a flaming candle. "What is it?" she asked.

Teacher laughed. "Why, it's your birthday. Did you forget?"

The other five students and the teacher all burst into a song. "Happy Birthday, dear Chanbopha, Happy birthday to you!"

"Now blow out the candle and wish."

But Chan couldn't—she was crying too hard. It seemed that all the tears she had dammed up inside her were released. "What's the matter Chan? Have we done something wrong?" said the teacher.

"Oh, no, It's just so wonderful! No one has ever wished me Happy Birthday before."

They all crowded around her, patting and hugging. Then they explained about wishing as she blew out the candle and how her wish would come true.

"Don't tell anyone what you wish for though," added someone.

Chan thought for a moment then squeezed her eyes tight shut and wished. She blew one strong puff, the flame fluttered out, and everyone cheered.

On Winter break from school Ma took her to where she worked picking crab. It was a long walk through streets lined by houses and apartments, then shops and crowded sidewalks which melted into an industrial area. At one point a chain link fence topped with barbed wire sent a chill through Chanbopha's very soul and she stopped in her tracks. In an enclosed yard men, all in the same type of jump suits, wandered aimlessly. Behind them loomed a stone building with only slits for windows and Chan knew it was a prison.

Ma grabbed her elbow, "No, never stop here. Not even look."

Too late. Already men gathered on the other side, whistling, hooting and shouting bad things.

Chan jumped back. She may not have understood the words but there was no mistaking the expressions and gestures.

Chan ran to catch up to her mother who had gone on ahead. "Who are those people?"

"Bad men," Ma said still hurrying. "Criminals. Pass quick so they don't notice."

Chan trotted on, shaken by the episode. She had been imprisoned and it was a terrible thing. Why did Ma not have pity for those men? Life was so confusing and filled with problems whichever way she turned. Maybe not so much if Papa had stayed alive but who knew! If only Liu were here to talk to; she hadn't realized what a wise and calming influence he had been. Always there when she needed someone. Vuthy and Sovirak were too busy with their own school and working lives and Ma didn't need to hear her teenage daughter's problems when at last she seemed worry free. There had been a rumor that the refugee camp had closed down. If that were true where had all the refugees gone? Where had Liu gone?

The crab factory blocked their way and Chan was grateful to pass through that large open door to safety.

The noise hit her first. Blaring music, added to by a chorus of loud female chatter and the staccato clang of crab shells being flung into metal buckets. Then there was the fishy crab stink that closed her nostrils and made her gasp for breath. She doubted she could survive in such an environment for more than ten minutes.

Long tables filled the factory floor and women sat on either side, all identical in coveralls, hairnets and rubber gloves. Ma pulled two sets of everything from the bag she'd been carrying and gave one to Chan. "Put them on." She said. "Doesn't matter if they are too big, they'll keep you clean".

The top, being made for a much larger bosomed lady than slender Chanbopha, was baggy, and the lower apron went around her twice but, as Ma said, it would keep her clean. It was the hair net Chan hated. It made everyone ugly and she'd had enough of ugliness. She longed to be pretty like other teenagers. At least none of the kids from school would see her here.

They sat at the nearest table where Ma demonstrated what to do. Then they settled down to work.

Chanbopha had been sternly told she would receive no pay for the filled bucket she took to be weighed if the smallest chip of shell was found amongst the crab meat inside. Many times that day her work was turned back as unacceptable and, as she saw the hands of other women flashing through each cooked and chilled crustacean, she became more and more frustrated.

By midnight when her shift ended, arms aching and fingers sore despite the rubber gloves, she looked sadly at her small pay of five dollars. "Why so little?" she wailed to Ma.

"Like everything you must learn," Ma replied. But Chan was already planning as they strode through darkness past the empty prison yard where only cats shifted in the shadows.

That night she had nightmares populated by the leering faces she had seen that morning. These however morphed into the prison guards who had screamed at her in her Pol Pot prison camp so long ago and she awoke dreading the walk she must soon repeat.

This time she and Ma rushed past the prison fence attracting little attention and when she got to work, Chan went straight to the supervisor and asked her to point out her best crab picker. Then she went to that woman and introduced herself. "Please, you are so good. Will you teach me?"

The woman smiled and her hands flew.

Chan laughed, "More slowly please, for just a minute. You have magic hands I cannot see!"

The woman grinned, went slowly, and Chan learned.

She was making good money now, picking crabs each day after school and also often on weekends after working at the restaurant. Chan's English was so improved she got a better job at a better restaurant, the Shanghai Rose, where everyone treated her well.

"I am happy with your work and think you will be a very fine waitress." The manager had drawn Chan aside and she waited for what he had to say. "One thing I ask of you, that you change your name which is too difficult for our American clientele. Find something you like. Will you do that Chanbopha?"

His request replayed in her mind while families began coming in for early dinner. One couple had a small girl who could only just walk and as the parents arranged their seating the child tottered away from them. Chanbopha on her way with menus was run into by the little one who looked up with a big smile. So like Srey before the troubles, thought Chan.

"Brenda!" called the mother,

One more big smile up at Chanbopha and little Brenda precariously tottered back to her parents. One happy little American girl beginning her life," thought Chan watching her, "Like me," she added.

"My name is Brenda," she said to the manager later that evening.

"Good choice," he nodded.

CHAPTER THIRTY-SEVEN

School hours were almost a rest now as Chan was quick to learn and lack of time for homework proved little problem. It was lack of sleep that often made it difficult to keep her eyes open and sometimes, on her way home late at night, her body aching, she almost longed for the easier days in the refugee camp with Liu—and her dreams of Papa still intact.

With the addition of Vuthy's wages from the cafeteria where he worked nights as a cook, their bank account was growing. Sovirak didn't like to work, only now and again joining his mother and sister to pick crabs, but as he was getting good marks in school and was chosen for the volley ball team no one complained. Chan however often wished to herself that he'd help around the house, but he had always been lazy except for in school. Being top of his class in math made Ma so proud she could never scold him. Chan was also top of her class, except in English, but Ma never mentioned that.

A month before final graduation Chan tapped on the principal's open door.

"Come in, Chanbopha."

How does she know my name, thought Chan, as she entered the room most students were only sent to for punishment of some heinous crime. It had taken all her courage to do this but Miss Robinson didn't look nearly as frightening sitting down as she did standing in front at roll call each morning. In fact she was actually smiling as she pulled out three files and looked them over. "You and your brothers have done very well." She pushed her glasses up on her forehead and leaned back in her chair. "You will soon leave us and what will you do then? College?"

"Thank you, but I think we will not have time for four years of college, we must work and become successful adults," said Chan. "But Mrs. Robinson, we missed so much early school, I want to ask you to let us stay here one more year. Please? We need this."

"Most students are eager to leave."

"Yes, Mrs. Robinson, but at first we learned little as our English was so small. One more year? Please?"

"I'll see what I can do and let you know." Mrs. Robinson stood up and came around to Chan. "You're a good girl, Chanbopha. You will be successful, I know. Perhaps the Thomas Nelson School of Business would be good? We will see when the time comes."

Chan muttered her thanks and stood, about to leave. "Mrs. Robinson?"

"Yes, Chanbopha?"

"At the restaurant where I work on weekends I am now allowed to wait on tables. But they said my name, Chanbopha, is too difficult for American customers so I now have a new name."

The principal waited with eyebrows raised.

"Brenda. They said it is a nice name. Is it, Mrs. Robinson?" Chan could not stop the choke in her voice. How could this stern American woman know how it felt to lose the name that had always been "you" during terrible years and was now cast off as she became someone new running toward a better life?

But maybe this school principal did understand for she leaned forward and lightly touched Chan's cheek with a forefinger. "Brenda is a beautiful name and I will sign you up as that for the Fall classes. I am proud to have you in my school, Brenda."

A letter arrived from the school two days later stating that due to special circumstances Brenda, Vuthy and Sovirak Oum would be accepted back to repeat grade twelve.

The boys were not pleased but when their sister impressed the importance of having a basis from which to build a career beyond their present lowly status they grudgingly agreed. Besides, Sovirak was happy to have another year on the volley ball team.

The three of them watched their friends graduate then settled down to a summer of work.

Brenda waitressed at the Shanghai Rose full time and after her shift walked the three miles to the crab picking factory. She worked there until midnight when the place closed for the cleaning crew to come in. Ma had changed to the 9 AM shift which meant Brenda had to walk home alone unless Vuthy decided to work that night. He tried to as often as possible and she knew he only cut hours at his much better paying real job because he worried about her. His fingers were not nimble enough to earn good money crab picking.

"Please, Vuthy, just do your own work. Stay with your good job. You hate doing this." They had reached home after a long day and stood outside their building. "I am grateful how you look after me but I'll be all right. Better you make more money to go to college." That was Brenda's goal for the family now. They must all get a business education followed by good jobs so Ma could stop working.

"You're sure you don't mind walking all that way home at midnight?" said Vuthy, but she saw the relief in his face as she nodded.

The summer heat lingered under their feet as they climbed the stairs to their apartment.

As Vuthy put his hand on the door knob Brenda stopped him. "Better not tell Ma. She'd only worry."

"Put this in your handbag then, it's pepper spray."

Brenda just had time to stuff the object into her handbag when the door burst open. "Come in and eat—dinner is waiting."

"But, Ma, It's one in the morning!" Brenda sniffed. "It does smell good though!" All Chan wanted to do was sleep but she knew preparing this meal was necessary for Ma so she not lose her importance in the family.

"Where's Sovirak?" asked Vuthy as they sat down at the table.

"Oh, he sleep. Come home late from computer programming class. He smart boy." Ma smiled proudly through steam of the soup she served.

And Vuthy is kind, thought Brenda. smiling at her step brother, like Liu, he was kind too.

CHAPTER THIRTY-EIGHT

That summer was so hot plunging her hands into the ice to pull out crabs was an anticipated relief but, later in the middle of the night, what had once been a solitary walk home with imagined fears was now rampant with real dangers. These were not from the prison which was locked down well before dark, but because of the heat which caused people to stray into the streets unable to sleep in their hot bedrooms. Men sat on front steps drinking beer and Brenda felt them watching her as she hurried past. Sometimes they called out but she tried not to listen.

With Indian summer Brenda could look forward to the start of school in a couple of weeks. No more having to work these late hours, she thought as she hurried homeward on this September night, bone tired but excited about showing Ma and Sovirak the envelope of money she had received for the most crabs she had ever picked in one day. A song even pursed her lips as she passed a group of teenagers hunkered around a lamp-post a bit away from the last house on the street.

As she stepped off the curb the biggest one blocked her way. Her nostrils filled with the acrid smell of him and she felt the presence of his friends encircling her.

"Move!" she said, putting her hands out to push her way through.

"We are the toll takers," said the boy grinning down at her.

"What toll?" said Chan, angry at having her good feelings destroyed.

"Toll to cross the street. New law for every foreigner—Chink especially. All the money you have will do. I know you work down that way 'cause I seen you passing before. I reckon you been paid today, Give it up and you can go home to your bowl of noodles."

Anger rose to the brim in Chan. These mountain sized thugs were not going to take the best day's earnings she'd ever had. She let her hand slide into the mouth of her handbag.

"Ah, good decision," The thug danced a toothpick between his lips.

Her fingers remembered and found the cylindrical shape, eased off the cap and found the nozzle. "Okay," she sighed, as though relinquishing hope, "Here you are."

The boys were all in front of her now, greedy eyed and pleased with themselves. As her hand left the bag, for a moment she saw the cruel faces of Pol Pot soldiers and all her hatred for them boiled up inside her. This time she could fight back.

She hit them in the eyes with the stream of pepper spray, squeezing and squeezing until it quit. Then she flung the metal tube with all her might into the nearest face.

Brenda ran, effortlessly, empowered by her victory and the yowls left behind her. Up the stairs she sprang to her apartment only a few blocks away and pushed through the door ready to throw her earnings on the table. But instead Ma rushed toward her, already talking. "Liu phoned. He's in California and he wants to come here to live with us!"

"Liu? In America?" Chan could barely speak. All these years he had been a phantom—a memory of a long ago time and world. "How did he find us?" It had almost come out as "me"

"He's in Oakland, California. A cousin sponsored him. I must ask this sponsor if he'll permit Liu to join us." Ma finally noticed the envelope Chan held and took it, spilling the bills onto the table. "Ah, well done Daughter. I never brought home this much."

Ma's seldom given praise thrilled Chan so that with news of Liu on top of it she never mentioned the attack on her way home. Instead she smiled wider than she'd had the energy to in a long time.

She sat, barely noticing what was on her plate. Liu is coming! Liu is coming! was all she could think. Her last thought before she went to sleep that night was to wonder if she and Liu would recognize each other.

Chan was not bothered on her way home again. The hot weather became cool, letting people sleep, and when vacation ended, school began and Chan only worked at crab picking when the restaurant was closed on Mondays. She went earlier, right after her last class, and any catcalls from the prisoners as she passed became almost a friendly greeting and Chan would wave back. After all she knew what it was like to be trapped where you didn't want to be.

At Shanghai Rose tips were not shared so, being popular with the patrons, Brenda did well and almost made up for not crab picking every night.

Always she waited for news of Liu. At home she listened for the telephone and when it rang she ran for it only to be disappointed. She kept remembering things about him. His strong slender fingers when he showed her how to squeeze a tire back onto the rim of his bicycle. The crinkle of a frown when he concentrated over the lessons she tried to teach him after school. How he hung up the hammocks every morning and said, "There!" as though he had produced a whole new room for them to enjoy. Why didn't he or his sponsor call?

Sometimes she wondered how they could have left him there continuing to live in that camp she had dreamed of escaping. She knew it was because she was young and too consumed with getting her family to America to think about it. After all he had always seemed so in charge of everything. But still...

She had just gotten home one night when it happened. She picked up the receiver. "Hello?"

"Chanbopha." For a moment there was silence.

"Is that really you, Liu?" Where had her voice gone.

"I told you I would find you. I have a plane booked for late night Saturday. Arrives Norfolk airport Sunday. Is that all right?"

"Of course. I am very happy." She felt suddenly shy.

"You don't sound like a little girl anymore," said Liu.

"I'm not. Here's Ma." And she handed the phone over to her mother.

That was Liu on the other end. The boy who once said he loved her. He was a man now. He will have changed. He may have a girlfriend. Doubts and fears galloped through Chan's mind.

She heard her Ma say they would meet him; repeat time of arrival, noon Sunday.

That night Chan had a nightmare. She was back in the refugee camp waiting on their doorstep for Liu to return from work at the embassy. A boy ran up and she recognized him as one who had tried to steal her crab picking money. This time he gave her something and ran away laughing. Chan looked at the note in her hand. "New Jersey Plane crash. Liu Dead." The shock of Papa's death two days before their reunion returned and Chan's own wail awoke her. She was afraid to go back to sleep...

CHAPTER THIRTY-NINE

School was easy this term having been through it all before. Her classmates didn't know that and admired Chanbopha's correct, only slightly accented answers. Some even asked her for help which she was happy and proud to give. Today she was only giving class half her attention.

Sony had offered to drive them to the airport to pick up Liu and the night before Chan had stood in front of the bathroom mirror and scrutinized herself. Still small and slight, but more curves. Her hair fell around her high cheek-boned face, the plaits long gone, and she could imagine she resembled Audrey Hepburn. Not as tall of course; but with that lipstick she'd bought yesterday from Woolworths... Oh she hoped he still liked her!

The plane was late and the Oum family waited in the lobby where they had arrived so full of hope four years earlier. Flight 453 had set down. They crowded among others, eagerly watching as the door at the far end of the room opened and passengers swarmed through. Chan stood on tiptoe although there was no one to see over. Every man she saw was Liu—for a moment—then he was met by others or strode purposefully on by. She wanted to cry. Had he changed so much she couldn't recognize him! Liu was not here! Then there he was striding toward them with that same wide smile. Those same kind eyes. And still so thin. He came straight to her, taking her hands and looking into her face. "I told you I'd find you," he said and with one gentle finger he traced the same letters on her cheeks and brow as he had that day long ago when she was still a child. This time she knew what they said.

EPILOGUE

Six months later Brenda graduated from high school and Liu and she married. It was a beautiful joyous ceremony with many in the Cambodian community attending.

The young couple moved into their own small apartment while Brenda attended business school during the day and worked in a restaurant at night. Liu, who took the name Tom, also worked in a restaurant and soon rose to be manager. They saved every possible penny and, armed with Brenda's business degree and Tom's experience, always looking forward, never back, after two years moved to California. There they bought a specialty donut shop which became popular and successful. With three strong, beautiful, intelligent daughters they moved to the best school district they could find and opened Papillon Gourmet Coffee, selling the Donut shop to Vuthy and his new wife. Sovirak is a computer programmer in Florida and Ma returned to a small village in Cambodia where she lives happily in the large house her daughter had built for her. As always Brenda looks ahead, finding ways to accomplish each new goal knowing that even though sometimes it seems impossible, nothing really is.

And there is now a very fine tombstone on her soldier father's grave.

Today as Brenda looks around her at the affluent customers she welcomes to Papillon each morning she tries not to think of the child who grew up eating rats and snake meat, wild herbs and grass. The little girl who saw death and beatings all around her but whose only thought was to get her family through it all—to the United States and Papa who would have a good life waiting for them.

But also Brenda does not want the Pol Pot and their evil ever to be forgotten. Always their kind will attempt to rise again and it is imperative that the knowing and watchful are prepared to stop them.

Brenda serves another latte and laughs at a customer's joke. Surely all that about the child called Chanbopha, must have been in a book she once read. She smiles at Tom, her Liu, and he, always close by, smiles back.

THE END

Oum family: (l-r) Sophia, Amy, Brenda, Ellen, Tom

Brenda Oum, 2015

ABOUT THE AUTHOR

Vancouver Island native Jil Plummer has trained horses in England, acted off-Broadway in New York City, worked on a banana plantation in Jamaica, and coordinated a clown show on ABC in Hollywood. While married to a photojournalist she traveled on many assignments throughout the world. She has also taught English as a second language. Jil has published three books (Remember to Remember, Caravan to Armageddon and Amber Dust) and has many more stories to tell.

For more information, please visit: www.jilplummer.com.

Made in the USA
Lexington, KY
22 April 2017